Jessup only trusts a few people, and he's perfectly fine with that. After the way his parents hurt him, he doesn't need anyone but his friends in his life.

He especially doesn't need a mate.

Rory has no idea what's happening. He was at the grocery store, and now he's locked up in a van with two other terrified people. He wants out and is ready for anything.

Except meeting his mate.

During a raid, Jessup notices a van and finds his mate inside. Rory is about to end up in the lab, and the thought terrifies Jessup as much as giving Rory a chance does. So Jessup doesn't.

Rory isn't easily deterred. Jessup is avoiding him, but he's already planning to move to Jessup's town, and as long as Jessup doesn't tell him to fuck off, he's not going anywhere. There are hurdles to deal with, though, like how a group of humans who call themselves hunters are supplying people to the labs and Jessup's fear that after being abandoned by his family, his mate will do the same.

Luckily, Rory is as stubborn as they come.

Jessup
Copyright © 2023 Catherine Lievens
ISBN: 978-1-4874-3857-9
Cover art by Angela Waters

Published by eXtasy Books Inc

Look for us online at:
www.eXtasybooks.com

Jessup
Mutants 3

By

Catherine Lievens

CHAPTER ONE

"Everyone knows the plan," Moore said, looking around the room. "Like always, if you don't feel up for it, let me know, and we'll find a way around it. I don't want anyone to do anything they're not ready for."

Jessup stayed silent, like everyone else in the room. No matter how horrifying what they'd find in this lab would be, they all wanted to be there. They knew what those people were going through, how much pain and horror they felt. They'd been in their place, and no matter how hard it was, they were ready to do whatever they could to save people from having to go through that again.

Moore nodded, clearly satisfied. "All right. Take a few minutes. We'll be ready to go as soon as everyone is done saying goodbye."

Jessup leaned back in his chair as the people around him got to their feet. They never knew what would happen during their missions, and it made sense for the mated mutants to spend a few minutes with their mates before leaving. Jessup didn't have to think about anyone but himself since he wasn't even dating anyone, and while that made the situation easier, he couldn't deny that seeing Moore with Jolyn and Hayes with Rikar made him a bit jealous. Would his turn ever come?

He sighed and got to his feet. Even if his turn did come, he didn't need a mate. He had plenty of things to live for and people he cared about, and really, what would he do with a mate?

He peered at Rikar and Hayes, who were sitting next to

him, their heads close together as they talked. Normally, Rikar wouldn't be at this meeting since he wasn't a mutant, but he was the leader of the tribe with which the mutants lived, and of course, he was Hayes's mate. That probably meant more than anything else to the people in the room. The fact that he'd welcomed them when they didn't have a home was also one of the reasons the mutants trusted him.

"I'll be here when you come back," Rikar promised.

Jessup stepped back, but instead of slipping away quietly, he bumped into Teddy. That would have been fine if Teddy hadn't tripped on a chair, drawing everyone's attention, including Hayes's and Rikar's.

"Everything all right?" Rikar asked as he studied Teddy.

Teddy nodded. "I'm fine, I'm fine."

"He was distracted by your kissy faces," Jessup said.

Hayes glared at him, but Rikar seemed to find it amusing. "Was he? Maybe he was jealous that we have someone to make kissy faces to."

Like always, he'd seen right through Jessup. Jessup had to resist the urge to glare at him, but even if he did glare, Rikar wouldn't care. They were becoming friends, mostly through Hayes, but why they were becoming friends didn't really matter. They were in each other's lives to stay, considering they both cared about Hayes, and that was okay.

Sometimes, though, Jessup wished Hayes could have a less perfect mate. Hayes made everyone jealous, including Jessup, who knew it was better for him not to find his mate anytime soon.

It wasn't just the mate thing, either. Hayes had many things Jessup wanted, and sometimes, he wondered if Hayes knew how lucky he was. He'd spent time in a lab like all of them, and he'd come out a little different, but he'd had a family before and still had them. They'd looked for him the entire time he'd been gone, and they'd been happy when he'd come back.

His mother wasn't dealing very well with the fact that Hayes wanted to work with the mutants, but she'd come around, especially since Hayes and Rikar had adopted a little girl.

But Jessup didn't have any family. He didn't have anyone but the mutants he considered brothers and sisters, which he supposed was okay. Sometimes, though, it was odd to realize that he didn't have anyone from before, when he'd been a normal shifter. The few people he cared about back then hadn't cared about him the same way, and they'd barely noticed he'd been gone. He hadn't gone back afterward and had no intention of ever doing so. His place was with the mutants now, and he was fine with that.

Most of the time.

"Do you have anyone to say goodbye to?" Rikar asked.

He sounded worried, but then he always did. There was always something or other that wasn't going the right way, and as a good tribe leader, it fell on his shoulders to take care of it. He was good at it, too, but realizing Hayes was his mate and bonding with him had made things worse. Rikar was worried more than ever about what would happen when the mutants went on missions. Still, he hadn't asked Hayes to stop, which made Jessup respect him even more.

Jessup still wished Rikar hadn't singled him out. He didn't want to talk about his loneliness and the fact that he didn't have anyone but the mutants. It would only remind him of all of it, and right before a mission, that was the last thing he needed.

"Is everyone ready?" Moore called out.

Jessup could have kissed him, although he suspected that Moore's mate wouldn't have been happy with that. Instead, he nodded curtly at Rikar, stood up straighter, and turned his attention to the leader of the mutants.

The people in the room were tense, but it wasn't different from any other day they had a mission. The moments before they shimmered there and snuck into the labs were the worst. There was a lot of waiting, anticipation, and worrying. Soon it would all be over, and they'd be coming home before they would even realize it.

But first, they had asses to kick.

The urge to shift made Jessup's skin crawl, but he ignored it as Moore started giving orders. They never took all the mutants on a mission. Everything depended on what they expected to find there, where the lab was located, and when they attacked. Jessup was usually present, but that was because of his mind control ability. He could have raided the labs on his own, although it wouldn't have been easy. The more people he had to control, the harder it was. It was even harder if he had to take them out, and while he controlled them with his mind, he was vulnerable to physical attacks. That was why he needed people with him, even though he hated that they put themselves in danger to protect him.

He couldn't make that decision for them, and they all knew what they were doing. He stepped away from Hayes and Rikar, giving them another few seconds, but soon, it was time to go.

They filed out of the room they used to meet, the tension greater and the silence heavy. Not many of them were leaving loved ones behind, but even those who weren't, like Jessup, were nervous. They had good info on most of the labs, but that didn't mean everything always went smoothly. If anything, the opposite was true. It was too easy for something to go wrong, and when that happened, it was a disaster. They hadn't lost any mutants yet, but they lost some of the people they were trying to rescue every so often, which made Jessup feel like shit.

He needed to get his head in the game, so he focused on the information Moore had given him and the others.

They were raiding the lab during the night, which meant

that while there would be guards, it would only be a skeleton crew. The labs often did that during the night, which Jessup thought was stupid, but he wasn't in charge of those places. If he was, he'd have more guards during the night because even though the people they experimented on were usually asleep then, the people on the outside wanting to save them weren't.

But attacking during the night also meant they'd have to deal with fewer civilians. Jessup didn't see a problem with killing the scientists who were experimenting on the people they caged, but now that the mutants were somewhat working with the council, they needed to capture the scientists, not kill them. The council wanted answers, which Jessup understood, but he'd been through this before. He'd come out of it with a new ability, and while it was handy, he still resented the scientists who'd hurt and tortured him for so long.

That was why he worked with Moore and the others. It was why he ran to the rescue every time he could.

Because he'd been where those people were, and he'd needed to be rescued. He, better than a lot of people, could understand.

The back of the van was completely dark. The windows had been covered, which meant that Rory couldn't see through them. He doubted he'd see anything interesting if he did, but it would give him hints as to where he was, which he needed to know.

He looked around the back of the van, trying not to be obvious about it. His gaze crossed with the gaze of the woman locked up with him. They stared at each other for a moment, and Rory felt a kind of kinship he'd never experienced.

Of course, he'd never been kidnapped and locked up in a van, so it probably made sense that he'd never felt that way.

The woman leaned closer. Her gaze flicked to the three men sitting up front, but they were bickering with each other and focused on the road. "My name is Alma," she whispered.

Rory nodded. "Rory."

"This is Benedict," Alma said, tilting her chin toward the man huddled against the side of the van next to her.

"Do you know what's happening?"

Alma shook her head. "They took me from the parking lot of the college I go to. That was two days ago, I think."

Rory looked down at Benedict, but he doubted the man would tell him anything. He was terrified, and the emotion seemed to be too much for him to deal with. Benedict was almost catatonic.

No, if Rory needed help escaping, he'd have to ask Alma. He wouldn't go down without a fight, whatever the consequences. The men who'd taken him from the grocery store parking lot didn't have anything good in mind. They wouldn't have grabbed him and thrown him in this van otherwise. Whatever they'd planned would no doubt end in pain.

"So you don't know where they're taking us?" Rory asked, just to be sure.

"I have no idea."

Rory nodded. He was thinking about what their next step would be. Wherever these men were taking them, they'd have to find a way to get out before they would force them into another vehicle, or worse, into whatever place they were about to reach. Rory had watched enough TV series about serial killers and whatnot to know that if they managed to get them to a secondary location, it was the end. He was ready to defend himself and even die in the process. He wasn't quite sure the same went for Alma and Benedict, but he supposed he'd find out soon enough.

He leaned even closer, keeping his voice barely more than

a whisper. "I'm going to fight them when they open the doors."

Alma frowned. Her dark hair hung around her face, half-hiding it from Rory. "They'll hurt you."

"What do you think they'll do once they get us wherever we're going? They didn't take us to be friends. I don't know about you, but I don't want to find out what they're planning."

"Shut the fuck up!" one of the men in the front suddenly yelled.

Rory jerked back, his heart racing at the thought that they'd been caught. He glanced at the man. Sure enough, the one in the middle had turned in his seat and was glaring at him.

Rory glared right back. He didn't care what the man thought or if he hit him. He was going to hurt Rory, anyway.

"You're a feisty one," the man said. For some reason, those words gave Rory the creeps.

The man driving laughed. "He's not going to be feisty for long. You know what they do to them."

Rory perked up. "Who docs what to who?"

"Shut up," the man in the middle snapped.

Rory was smart enough to know it would be better if he obeyed. He knew who he'd try to hit once he was out of here, though. That guy deserved to get his ass beaten.

"What did you have in mind?" Alma asked after a few moments.

Rory looked around. There was nothing in the back of the van except for him, Alma, and Benedict. These guys had been smart enough to use one of those collars on all of them, which meant that even though Rory was a shifter and suspected the same went for Alma and Benedict, none of them would be able to shift. He wouldn't have been able to do much in his animal form, but it still would have been easier than attacking in his human form. He had no idea how to do that, but he was

7

going to have to find a way, and soon because he could feel the van slowing down.

He swallowed. "I'll throw myself at whoever opens the van," he told Alma.

Her eyes were wide, but she nodded. "They're not going to take it kindly."

"Do I look like I care? Because I don't. I'll kick their ass, and they'll regret kidnapping me." Rory's groceries were probably all ruined by now. He wasn't rich, dammit, and he couldn't afford to get more stuff.

But he'd think about his groceries later. The van was slowing more and more, and when Rory felt it stop, he knew the time had come. He and Alma looked at each other again, and she nodded. Whatever happened next, she was ready to fight with him, and while Rory was pretty sure both of them would be hurt by the end of this, at least they weren't giving up.

They couldn't afford to.

Rory hooked his fingers on the collar around his neck. He pulled, but there was no removing it, and it was too late now anyway. The men had climbed out of the van, and the back door slowly opened. Rory crouched, ready to defend himself, Alma, and Benedict.

Whatever that meant.

Once the door was open enough, he screamed and launched himself forward. The man behind the door made a surprised sound, but Rory didn't let that stop him. He threw himself at him, trying to scratch the man's face, arms, and whatever else he could reach. The problem was that the man was clearly used to all of this, and Rory's hands were tied together. The man didn't hesitate to grab one of Rory's arms and push him away, and when Rory stumbled back, a well-placed punch was enough to knock him down.

"That wasn't smart," the man snarled.

Rory glared at him. "No one ever said I was smart."

"You really aren't. It's going to be fun to find out what they do to you."

Rory wanted to know who the *they* these guys were talking about were, but he suspected he wouldn't like the answer and that it was better for him not to ask. "Let us go," he ordered, even though he knew it wouldn't work.

"What's taking so long?" another man asked.

"This one tried to attack me," the guy Rory had rushed whined.

Rory was tempted to attack him again. What would happen if he did? He could imagine this guy beating him up, and while he wasn't looking forward to that happening, he was starting to think that maybe, it would be better. Rory had seen enough of those serial killer series to be able to come up with about a dozen things that might be about to happen to him and the other two.

No more TV for him if he ever made it back home.

The guy reached into the van, clearly intent on dragging Rory out. Rory didn't think he could win this, but he could make it as hard as possible. He plastered himself far away from the door, glaring at the man who had to step into the van to get to him.

Rory could tell only a few things, like the fact that the guy was human. Why would three humans take him and another two shifters? What were they planning to do?

The man grinned as he reached for Rory, but to Rory's surprise, it didn't last long. The man's eyes widened, and he was pulled out of the van. He went with a shout that quickly cut out, and Rory listened, holding his breath.

He couldn't hear the three men anymore. What he *could* hear was the sound of someone fighting, and he had no idea what it meant.

Something heavy hit the side of the van from the outside, startling Rory and pushing him to move away. It brought him closer to the door, and even though he was terrified, he wasn't about to stay there and wait for whatever was happening outside to be over. It might be his only chance to escape.

A man appeared at the van's door before Rory could step out. Rory tensed, expecting the man to drag him out, but before either of them could say anything, a gust of wind pushed the man's scent toward Rory.

What the fuck? Had Rory's mate kidnapped him?

When Jessup peeked inside the van, it was to see three figures huddled as far away from the door as they could. He wasn't surprised. He might not have known anything about the van he and the others had noticed parking at the back of the lab, but he had a good imagination, and he'd been in one of these before.

Just like the other mutants, he'd been taken from his life, locked up in a van, and brought to one of the labs. That had to be what had happened to these people, and Jessup felt deeply satisfied at the thought that he and the other mutants were helping them.

He'd known something was happening when he'd seen the van. Thankfully, Moore had agreed and had sent him and a few others to free the people in the van. It had been easy. Jessup and the others only had three humans to take on, and with the way they trained, it had only taken them a few minutes.

Jessup wasn't sure what to do with the humans now, though. He wanted to go inside the lab and help the others, but at the same time, he also wanted to stay and protect the people in the van.

He leaned forward, intent on talking to one of them. Maybe he could find out where they'd come from. The goal was always to reunite these people with their families, and if there was no one to reunite them with, like in Jessup's case, to find them a safe place to settle down. Most of the people who survived the labs had long recoveries ahead of them, and they couldn't exactly go back to their old lives as if nothing had happened to them.

Jessup would know. He'd tried.

One of the men placed himself in front of the other two people in the van. Jessup was impressed that even though he was terrified, he was ready to stand up for his friends. Jessup raised his hands, intent on showing the man he wasn't a danger.

That was when the smell hit him.

The inside of the van reeked of fear and sweat, but even with that, Jessup could smell his mate. He was pretty sure it was the guy in front, although it could be the one huddled in the back, too. Hopefully, it wouldn't be the woman. Jessup had nothing against women and loved several, but not the way he should love a mate. His orientation went to guys, and hopefully, Fate knew that.

Jessup swallowed. What was he supposed to do? He hadn't expected to meet his mate and had no idea how to deal with it. He couldn't exactly tell the guy they were fated to be together. If the man was a shifter, he probably knew it already, anyway. Besides, Jessup needed to stop wasting time. These people would be safe as soon as he and the others took care of the humans in the facility. Jessup didn't need to stay here. He had to go to his friends and make sure they were okay.

"Watch out!" Teddy yelled.

Jessup turned in time to grab the fist coming toward his face. The man who'd been trying to drag Jessup's mate out of the van stood there, apparently stunned that Jessup had managed to stop him. Jessup rolled his eyes, then punched the man in the face. The man went down with a whimper, then stopped moving, but Jessup wasn't done. He needed to make sure this guy wouldn't get up again. He'd thought putting him to the ground once had been enough, but clearly, he'd been wrong.

So Jessup leaned over the man and punched him again. There was no reaction this time, a sure sign the man was unconscious. Jessup nodded at himself, satisfied with his work, then looked up at Teddy, who was bleeding from his lower lip.

Jessup swore, rushed to his friend, and sighed. "What happened?"

Teddy shook his head. "I didn't see the third one. I'm sorry."

"You have nothing to be sorry about. I should have been more careful." And he would have if he hadn't realized one of the guys inside the van was his mate. "The guy we caught?"

"The one I was fighting with ran away, along with the third one we didn't notice. We only have this one left."

Jessup nodded and poked at the guy with his booted foot. "He'll do." They'd get information out of him, which was the only reason Jessup hadn't killed him. Whoever this guy was, he'd kidnapped Jessup's mate. He'd have to pay for that.

Teddy needed a moment, so Jessup focused on tying up the man and sending Leon and Davey after the other two. He texted Moore to let him know what had happened, even though Moore wouldn't see the text until the lab was secure. Once Teddy gathered himself, he shimmered the man back to the village, where the mutants they'd left behind would ensure he couldn't run away. Whoever this guy was, he was their prisoner now, which meant he wouldn't like what was about to happen to him.

By the time Teddy came back, Jessup was anxious. The three were still in the van, and he had no idea what to do. Should he go in and tell them everything was all right? Would they believe him if he did?

"What now?" Teddy asked.

Jessup looked from the lab to the van. Moore hadn't answered, and it made him nervous. "I'm going to go inside and make sure everyone's all right. They're going to need my ability."

Teddy nodded. "What about the people inside the van?"

"I'm sure they'd rather talk to you than to me. You're much cuter."

Teddy rolled his eyes, but they both knew it was the truth. He was a Nix, which meant that between his pointed ears, green eyes, and blond hair, he was adorable and looked about as dangerous as a kitten. Many people had fallen for that, which always made Teddy roll his eyes. It was good that people tended not to see him for how he really was until it was too late.

"I'll stay with them," he promised.

"I know you will. I'll be back as soon as possible, and if I can't come, I'll send someone. Do what you can to reassure the people in the van that they're all right." Jessup hesitated, but he couldn't tell Teddy that one of them was his mate. He wasn't even sure he could accept it himself or that he'd ever be able to. "And when Leon and Davey come back, keep one of them with you and send the other in."

Teddy didn't seem to notice anything was wrong. He nodded and moved toward the van, and even though Jessup wanted to stick around and officially meet his mate, he knew better. Moore and the other mutants needed him, and his place was with them.

Jessup made himself move toward the lab. He could sneak in from the back, where the van had been parked. There was a door there, but the electronic lock wasn't engaged anymore. None of them were now that the mutants were in the lab.

Jessup opened the door and peeked into the hallway. It was

empty, but he could hear people screaming somewhere close. He cracked his knuckles, ready to throw himself into the fight and forget about his mate, at least for now. It wasn't something he'd be able to ignore, especially if his mate had smelled him and knew about their bond, but for now, it felt good to ignore it and focus on the mission.

Jessup prowled down the hallway, ready to act. He didn't have to walk far to find an opportunity. Two guys in white coats were in one of the rooms Jessup checked, feeding documents through a shredder. Jessup stopped that right away, blocking them with his ability. He could hold them there for a while if he had to, but he didn't want to get too tired, just in case, so he had one of them tie the other up to a chair, then took care of the second one. He kept them calm as he texted Moore again to warn him, then sent them to sleep so he could continue.

This he knew how to deal with and how to accomplish. His mate, though? He wouldn't know where to begin.

Rory was confused. He was pretty sure the guy who'd saved him was his mate, but instead of coming toward him, his mate had turned around and left. He hadn't even talked to Rory, which worried him for a moment. Then the blond guy stepped into the van, and Rory focused on protecting Alma and Benedict.

The man raised his hands. The only light in the van came from outside, but the man was close enough to the door that Rory could see him fairly well. He identified him as a Nix, which the guy wasn't trying to hide since his ears were exposed. The man raised his hands like Rory's mate had, but he didn't move away.

"Hi," the man said. "My name is Teddy. I know you're confused and wondering what's going on, but I wanted to let you know that you're safe."

Rory wanted to believe him, but could he? "What if you're lying?"

Teddy smiled softly. "I understand where you're coming from."

Rory snorted. "Have you ever been kidnapped from the grocery store parking lot, stuffed into a van, and threatened?"

"Yes. Well, it wasn't a grocery store, but my story is similar to yours. I was taken, stuffed into a van, and brought to one of the labs."

Rory swallowed. He was young, but not so young that he didn't know about the labs. "They're supposed to be a thing of the past."

"They are, and we're doing everything we can to make that happen."

"So — what, you're here to rescue us?"

"You and whoever we find inside the facility. You were lucky because we managed to keep you out of it. The people inside, though? They'll probably be in bad shape."

Rory shivered. He didn't want to believe Teddy, but his instincts were telling him he should. Teddy and Rory's mate hadn't had to help, but they'd stepped in, and apparently, they were helping a bunch of people Rory hadn't known about. It was too easy to imagine what would have happened to him and the others if they'd been taken inside the lab. Rory had heard the stories, and all of them were horrifying. The fact that Teddy had gone through that made him want to hug the guy, but he was pretty sure he stank. Besides, Teddy wasn't Rory's mate.

"What's the name of the guy who was with you?"

Teddy cocked his head, clearly puzzled. "Which one? There were four of us."

"The only one who came in." Rory wished he'd gotten a better look, but he'd been terrified. "He was tall, with short dark hair."

"I'm pretty sure you're talking about Jessup. What about him?"

"You work with him?"

"I do. Did he do or say something that scared you?"

Rory shook his head. "No. I was just curious." If Jessup worked with Teddy, it probably meant Rory would see him again. Maybe not tonight, considering what was happening just a few feet away, but eventually.

That was all Rory wanted. Right now, he didn't think he could deal with having met his mate, but that didn't mean he wanted to step away from the bond. Eventually, he'd want to find Jessup and talk to him.

"Well, why don't the three of you come out? Most of our group is inside the lab, so you don't have to worry about being overwhelmed."

Rory looked back at Alma and Benedict. Benedict had stopped shivering, but he still didn't look good.

"I think he needs medical help," Rory told Teddy.

Teddy turned his attention to Benedict. He didn't have to look for long, and from his grimace, he agreed with Rory. "I'll have someone called. You shouldn't worry, though. He'll be fine."

"I wish I could believe you, but honestly, after what happened to us, I'm not sure any of us will be fine."

Teddy nodded as if he understood, and apparently, he did. That meant he didn't push Rory or the other two to get out of the van, even though he clearly wanted nothing more. He gave them all the time they needed, and since Rory was terrified, it helped to focus on Alma and Benedict. That way, he didn't have to think of his own fear, which he suspected would knock him to his knees if he gave it a chance to.

He wasn't going to.

He took Alma's hand, startling her. She nodded at him, and

together, they got Benedict to his feet. Teddy still hovered close, but he didn't move to help them. That made sense because he didn't know how Benedict would react to his presence.

Benedict didn't even seem to notice. He allowed Alma and Rory to guide him toward the doors, then out of the van. Rory took a deep breath, then another, and took a moment to look around.

They were in the middle of trees, possibly a forest. The moon was high in the sky, and the many lights illuminating the parking lot meant that when he turned around, he could see the facility in which he'd almost ended up. It made him shiver in horror, and he leaned closer to Alma.

"How long have you been with these people?" Teddy asked.

"They took me tonight," Rory explained. "Several hours ago, I think. I lost track of time in that van."

"They got me a few days ago," Alma interjected. "But I don't know how long they had Benedict. I think it was longer than that because he was already in the van."

Teddy nodded, his expression telling Rory he wasn't surprised. "From what we've been able to find out, this is how the labs find the people they experiment on now. They have groups of humans that call themselves hunters go around the country, kidnap people, and bring them to the labs. It makes sense that they wait until they have two or three people before coming making their delivery."

Rory wrapped an arm around Benedict. He was pleasantly surprised when, instead of freaking out, Benedict leaned against him. They hadn't known each other long, but seeing Rory in the same position had clearly helped Benedict trust him.

"Jessup and Leon went back inside, and Davey is poking around the forest, trying to find the two guys who escaped,"

Teddy continued. "But you're safe. We got the third guy, and he's our prisoner."

"Why do you keep them prisoner?" If it up to Rory, he'd torture them. He wasn't quite sure what that would look like because he got queasy at the sight of blood, but he'd find a way to do so while keeping all the blood inside. It had to be doable, right?

"Because hopefully, they have answers, and we need those. The labs are part of a network, and the more of them we find, the more people we can free."

It was terrifying to think there were more places like this, but considering how easy it had been for those guys to take Rory, Rory wasn't surprised.

"You don't know me, and you don't have a reason to trust me," Teddy said. "But I'd like to shimmer you back to the village where we live. There's medical help available for your friend and you if you need it."

"I want to go home," Alma said.

Teddy nodded. "You will. I'm not promising it'll happen tonight because I'm sure my leader will have questions for you, and he wants everyone to be checked out by healers, but probably tomorrow. As long as you have a place to go back to, we'll get you there. First, though, we'll take care of you, if you're okay with that."

Alma and Rory looked at each other, then Rory looked down at Benedict. He was still huddled against Rory's chest, seemingly not having heard anything Teddy had said. Maybe he had heard it but couldn't make sense of it, or maybe he wasn't even there. It was impossible to tell, but Rory wanted him to get medical help as soon as possible.

There was only one thing he and Alma could do, and that was to trust Teddy. Hopefully, they wouldn't regret it.

Rory turned back to Teddy. "All right. You can take us wherever you think we need to go."

Teddy nodded and held out his hand. "I'm a Nix, as you can see, so I'll take you to safety right away."

Alma took Teddy's hand while Rory clung to her other hand, holding it so tightly that it had to hurt. He'd never met Alma before tonight, but after what they'd gone through together, she felt the safest out of everyone here. Thankfully, she didn't have anything to say about how hard Rory squeezed her hand. He supposed she needed the contact, too, and that sticking together would make it easier to get through the next few hours.

CHAPTER TWO

Jessup had slept like shit. He wasn't surprised, and after what happened last night, he'd expected it. His mate was in town, and Jessup knew exactly where. All the survivors had been taken to the same house, where a healer saw them and where they could spend the first night.

The work wasn't over yet. Today, Jessup and the others would talk to everyone they'd rescued from the lab. They'd make sure they were okay, ask them what happened to them and about their families. They'd contact whoever they needed to contact and do their best to reunite families. That was the best part of the job, but it had never been the part Jessup looked forward to.

It hurt. He'd never had a family to reunite with, and even though he wanted these people to have what he didn't have, it didn't mean he wanted to see it happen time and time again. He usually tried to get out of it, and thankfully, Moore understood.

Could Jessup stay away this time? His mate would be there, probably wanting to talk to him. Jessup had asked Teddy how the three people they'd found in the van were, and Teddy had reassured him that they were all fine physically. He'd started talking about one of the guys, Benedict, and it had taken Jessup a while to realize that wasn't his mate. Benedict was the guy who'd barely moved, and while Jessup was glad he'd be okay, it didn't help him find out more about his mate. He had a name, at least. Teddy had mentioned all three people by name, so Jessup knew it was Rory.

Where did that leave him?

He should find his mate. If Rory was a shifter and had smelled Jessup, he'd know they were mates and wonder why Jessup was hiding from him. Jessup didn't want to hurt him, but he had no clue what to do with a mate. He barely knew what to do with his friends, and he only had them because they knew how awkward he was and didn't get offended easily. They ignored how he pushed them away sometimes, and they focused on being there for him. It wasn't something he'd had before, and he wasn't sure Rory would be ready to deal with the mess Jessup was, especially considering his ability.

It made people uncomfortable. Jessup didn't blame them, but there was nothing he could do. He could control people with his mind. Often, they didn't believe he'd never do that to them unless it was in a life-or-death situation. Why would he want to control his friends? Or people who'd never hurt anyone? He didn't have a reason to, but most people didn't seem to understand that. It was just easier to stay away and be on his own, but Jessup doubted he could do that when it came to his mate. At the very least, he'd have to talk to Rory.

He wasn't sure he was looking forward to that.

A sudden pounding on his door made him jump and scramble out of bed as if his ass were on fire. His heart raced as he glared at the door, ready to strangle whoever was behind it. "What?" he snapped as he eyed his bed.

He didn't want to leave it, but staying in wouldn't help him get more sleep, unfortunately. He'd been awake for hours, obsessing over his mate, and he doubted anything would change that. Maybe seeing Rory, but was that really what Jessup wanted? Could he deal with it?

"We have work to do," Leon said from the hallway.

He'd clearly been sent to get Jessup, which was never a good thing because he was one of those annoying people who got up with their alarm and were ready to face the day in minutes. Jessup, on the other hand, needed about an hour and several cups of coffee before he could blink his eyes open.

"And you had to pound the door down?" Jessup grumbled.

"I wanted to make sure you were awake. Are you awake?"

"I'm talking to you, asshole."

"But I can't see you."

"I'm awake, and I'm going to kick your ass if you don't leave me alone."

Leon laughed. "Fine. Moore expects us to start working soon, though. Come downstairs. You can grab coffee, we can talk about what's next, and maybe you can tell me why Olga told me to get you."

Jessup knew what was next. It was always the same, and neither he nor the other needed to talk about it again. Moore liked things done the right way and was a bit obsessive over it, especially since the mutants had started working with the council. They didn't take orders from them, but it was odd to think they had to answer to someone in a way. The council could stop the mutants, and no one was willing to let that happen, least of all Moore.

So instead of climbing back into bed and trying to go back to sleep while ignoring the fact that his mate was somewhere in town, Jessup went to shower and dress. He felt a little bit more human by the time he was done, which was a good thing. Coffee would help him get all the way there, but once breakfast was over, he wasn't quite sure what he'd be expected to do, especially if Olga had requested him specifically.

He'd find out soon enough.

Almost everyone was in the kitchen when he got there. Leon handed him a cup of coffee, which Jessup took with a glare that turned into a blissful expression after he took his first sip. No matter how annoying Leon was, he made good coffee.

"You should have gotten more sleep," Olga said from the table where she was eating cereal.

Jessup glared at her. "Thank you for letting me know. I would never have thought of it myself."

Instead of being offended, Olga grinned. "I know what the problem is."

Of course she did. Her ability meant she could see the future, but she almost never told anyone what she saw exactly. She hinted at things here and there and tended to push people into situations when she knew it would be good, but it made Jessup nervous. Did she know he'd met his mate? If she did, what would she do about it?

"I'm not doing anything you tell me to do," he warned.

Olga just grinned at him. "We'll see."

Jessup clutched his cup of coffee and stepped out onto the porch. He loved his people, but sometimes, he needed time on his own. He was already overwhelmed, and it was only breakfast.

The door opened and closed behind him, telling him someone had joined him. He stayed where he was, leaning on the railing and looking out at the forest.

"You're extra grumpy this morning," Leon said.

"What's it to you?"

"Well, you're a friend, so I want to know if something's wrong. There's also the fact that Hayes is going to kick my ass if I don't at least ask."

Jessup sighed. "I'm fine."

"Are you? Because no one will care if you're not. Rescuing people from the labs is hard on all of us. We do it because it's the right thing to do, but sometimes, it's natural to need to take a step back."

Jessup rubbed his face with his free hand. "I'm fine with going on the raids."

"Are you? Because something happened last night, and you don't seem to know how to deal with it."

Jessup had two options. He could tell Leon to fuck off, even though he was a friend. Leon would respect that, but he'd still be worried, and Jessup still wouldn't have anyone to talk to about his mate.

Or Jessup could tell Leon about Rory. That meant Leon might try to push him toward his mate, and Jessup wasn't sure if that would be good or bad. He'd have to talk to Rory eventually. He didn't know what he'd say, but Rory deserved a conversation at the very least, and Jessup wanted to give that to him. Rory had been through hell, even though he'd never been in the lab itself. Being kidnapped and thrown into a van was enough to give anyone nightmares, and Jessup wanted nothing more than to be there for his mate.

He sighed. If he was going to be there for Rory, he'd need someone to tell him how to do that because he was clueless. That someone might not be Leon, but maybe telling him would help Jessup feel better.

"You know those three people in the van last night?" he asked. He deliberately didn't look at Leon.

"What about them?"

Jessup sucked in a breath. "One of them is my mate."

Rory woke up panicking and out of breath. It took him a moment to recognize the room he was in, and when he did, he told himself to breathe and calm down.

He was safe. He wasn't home, but he was safe.

He sat up and gathered the blanket around his body. He shivered, although he wasn't sure he was cold. It didn't matter. He needed to feel more settled, and being wrapped in a blanket helped.

He licked his lips as he looked out the window. The sun

was up, but it didn't seem to be too late. It wasn't like he had anywhere to go. He hadn't realized it yesterday, but he'd been in that van for two days. Knowing his boss, that was probably enough to fire him, which meant he needed to find another job. He didn't mind. He'd worked there to pay his bills, but it wasn't like he loved it, especially considering how much of a dick his boss was.

It was just one more thing that hurt. He'd been kidnapped, taken to one of those horrible labs, and lost his job. How could his life have gone to shit so quickly?

But looking around the room, he reminded himself that it wasn't all bad. Yes, he'd probably have nightmares for years to come, but he hadn't been hurt physically, and he'd met his mate.

Well, kind of. He knew his mate's name and what he looked like, but for now, that was all. He hadn't seen Jessup again and wasn't sure how to make that happen. Should he ask someone? Maybe Rikar, the Nix who'd welcomed them when they'd arrived in this small town? He'd explained he was the leader of the tribe who'd built the place and the unofficial mayor. He took care of his people, and for now, Rory and the others who'd been recovered at the labs were his people.

Rory was almost afraid to leave his bed. He felt safe all alone in this small bedroom. He could hear people outside, talking quietly to each other, but he didn't want to see anyone. It wasn't that he was afraid they'd hurt him. He doubted that, considering they'd saved him. He was still terrified and didn't know how to deal with it.

Everything was a mess, and he did know where to start fixing his life.

He forced himself out of bed, knowing that staying there wouldn't help. He had to face what had happened and the consequences it would have, even though it would be so much nicer for him to hide. He wanted to check in on Benedict, though, and he couldn't do that from his bedroom. So he got up, showered, and put on the clothes he'd been given yesterday. He'd been glad to take off his own clothes, even though he'd been wearing his favorite t-shirt. It wasn't his favorite anymore, because every time he looked at it, it would remind him of what had happened.

The clothes he'd been given had been new but washed. They smelled of laundry soap — of home — which was odd, because he was nowhere near his home or his family. It helped settle him a bit more, though, and by the time he was ready, he felt like he could face whatever was waiting on the other side of his bedroom door.

He wanted answers, especially when it came to his mate, and he'd get them.

He was careful when he opened the door, but the hallway was empty. All the doors were closed, and he quickly walked past them, wondering if the people behind them felt like him. He hadn't seen much last night because the healer had told him to get some rest and go to bed after Rikar had given him food, but he knew that some of the people who'd been saved from the lab had been in bad shape. He didn't think all of them were here, if anything, because they'd needed medical attention. Benedict was one of those people, and Teddy had told Rory and Alma that they'd taken him to the clinic because the healer wanted to keep an eye on him overnight. Rory had been relieved. He wanted to help Benedict, but he wouldn't know where to start.

The smell of breakfast told him where the kitchen was. He'd been there last night, but he wasn't sure he'd have remembered its location, and he didn't want to wander the house like an idiot. When he walked into the room, he was surprised to see Rikar in front of the stove, but the sight of the Nix helped him relax. Rikar had been nothing but nice to him and the others, and something told Rory he was safe with him.

Rikar looked up when he heard him and smiled. "I wasn't sure when I'd see you."

"I wasn't sure I'd find the courage to leave my bedroom," Rory answered.

Rikar nodded as if he knew what Rory was talking about. "I can't say I've ever been through what you've been through, but I've seen enough people trying to recover from it. It won't be easy."

Rory shrugged. "I don't need it to be easy. I just need to get better."

Rikar flipped the pancake in the pan before turning his attention back to Rory. "How did you sleep?"

"With my eyes closed."

Rikar arched a brow.

Rory looked away and rubbed the back of his neck. "Sorry. I know you're trying to be nice, but it's hard not to push you away. I only met you yesterday, and I don't know if I can trust you." Rory wouldn't have hesitated normally, but he wasn't sure he could do this after what had happened to him.

He'd always given people the benefit of the doubt, and he'd never been afraid of most of them, but that had changed. He'd been kidnapped from a parking lot. How could he trust anyone after that?

Thankfully, Rikar didn't look offended. He slid the pancake onto a plate, then, to Rory's surprise, offered it to him.

"I can't take your breakfast."

"It's not mine. It's yours."

"You were cooking for me?"

"And for anyone else who wants breakfast. I don't live here, but I try to spend some time in this house in the days following a raid. You and the others need people to take care of you, and it's one thing I can do."

Rory sat at the table, thankful he wouldn't have to find something to eat by himself. He probably would have stuck to a cup of coffee and nothing more in that case. He started eating, but his mind wasn't on it. "Do you know the people who rescued me and the others last night?" he asked.

Rikar had sat on the other side of the table and was sipping on a cup of something that didn't smell like coffee. He lowered his cup, already nodding. "I do. If you want to know if you can trust them, you can. I doubt any of them told you their story, but I can tell you that they went through a lot, just like you. They know what you're going through, which is why they help."

"Teddy told me he was kidnapped, too." But he wasn't who Rory wanted to talk about. "I'm wondering about the others, though."

"Anyone in particular?"

Rikar wasn't going to make this easy. "Yes. His name is Jessup."

Rikar nodded, looking a bit surprised. "What do you want to know? I have to say I'm surprised you're asking about him. Teddy was the one who shimmered you here."

"But Jessup was the one who beat up the guys who'd taken me and the others."

"And you want to thank him for that?"

Rory glared. He understood why Rikar was asking questions, but did he have to make this so difficult? "I'd like to talk to him."

"Well, I'm sure that's going to happen eventually. The mutants don't leave the people they rescue on their own. They'll help you get home and make sure you have anything you need, including therapy."

Rory's mind was stuck on one word. "Mutants?"

Rikar waved Rory's question away. "You'll see them today. They'll want to know more about your life and what happened to you, and they'll make sure you get home. You don't have to worry about anything."

"I want to move here permanently."

Rikar blinked. "I'm sorry?"

"Jessup is my mate, which means that I need to move. He lives here, right?"

"He does, and congratulations. Shouldn't you talk to him before making that kind of decision?"

Rory supposed he should, but he felt like he'd lost control, and he needed to get it back. What better way than to make life-changing decisions? Besides, after what Rory had gone through and survived, he wanted to fight for what he desired.

That included his mate.

"I'm sure I can find something else to do," Jessup said, desperately trying to find a way out of visiting the survivors.

Moore stared at him as if he'd grown a second head. "What's up with you?"

"Nothing. I just didn't sleep well."

Olga snickered, and Jessup wondered if she'd see it if he decided to trip her. Probably, and she'd dance out of the way and make him look like an idiot. It was tempting to do it anyway, though.

"Well, you're grumpier than usual," Moore said. "Try not to scare any of the survivors. They don't need that after what they've been through."

Great. Now Jessup felt guilty. "I don't want to freak anyone out, which is why I should stay away."

"We might need you to help keep these people calm. I can see how conflicted you are, and I wouldn't ask you to be there if I didn't think we need you."

Jessup stared for a moment, then sighed. "I know. I'll stop."

"No more tantrums?" Leon asked.

Jessup glared at him. "It wasn't a tantrum."

Leon knew. Jessup had told him about Rory and how he'd run away without even talking to him. He knew Jessup was planning to avoid his mate because he didn't know what to do. Leon had pointed out that Jessup didn't need to make decisions right away, especially life-changing ones, and that, at the very least, Rory deserved to have a conversation with Jessup. Jessup agreed, but that didn't mean he'd go out of his way to make it happen. He was still freaking out and had no idea how to take care of a mate. Hell, his mate had been kidnapped and had almost ended up in a lab. What kind of person did that make Jessup?

The kind who was freaking out and terrified.

The house where the survivors stayed while they were in town was at the end of the street. It meant they had privacy, which was what they needed after what they'd gone through. They'd been told to expect the little group Jessup was part of. They might even recognize some of them, including Jessup. They'd been told someone would check in on them today, and here Jessup was, ready to do just that.

None of them were surprised when Rikar opened the door. He always visited the day after a raid to check in on the survivors. Even though he didn't know them, he viewed taking care of them as his responsibility.

Jessup looked around as soon as he stepped into the house. For some reason, Rikar was staring at him, and that made him want to run. Instead, he avoided looking at his best friend's mate and focused on the wall instead.

"Could I have a glass of water?" Olga suddenly asked.

Jessup knew she was planning something. He could see it in the twinkle in her eyes, and he was afraid it had something to do with him. It scared him more than the raids.

Rikar gestured them toward the kitchen. "Of course. One

of the survivors is in the kitchen right now, so maybe you can start with him."

"I'd love to," Olga said with a wide smile.

They all followed her and Rikar because what else could they do? Moore didn't seem to realize something was up, but Leon kept peeking at Jessup, and Jessup kept glaring at him. He had no idea what Olga was doing and didn't want to find out, but something told him he was about to. She was a meddler. She couldn't help herself, and after what had happened last night, Jessup had no doubt she knew something.

Sure enough, when he stepped into the kitchen, it was to find Rory sitting at the table, sipping on a cup of coffee. He looked up when he heard them, blinked, then focused on Jessup.

Jessup had to resist the urge to turn around and run away, possibly screaming. He stared back at Rory, not knowing what to do or say. Was there even anything he *could* do or say? Was Rory angry at him for not coming back sooner? Maybe for not staying with him in the van and leaving him with Teddy? There was no way for Jessup to know except ask, and he didn't plan to do that anytime soon. He hadn't planned to talk to Rory at all, but Olga had known this would happen, and she'd made sure Jessup would be here.

Dammit.

Rory shot to his feet, startling everyone. Jessup was frozen, and he watched as his mate walked around the table and came to stand in front of him. They stared at each other.

In Rory's eyes, Jessup could see his future. It was an odd sensation. He'd always thought he'd be alone, but Rory's presence meant he didn't have to be. Was that enough for him to give Rory a chance? What if he hurt Jessup?

He might. After all, the people Jessup had thought were his family had hurt him. They'd vanished from his life, abandoning him, and for a long time, he'd told himself it was for the best. He didn't need anyone.

That was a lie.

Everyone needed people, including Jessup. No matter how many times he told himself he was fine on his own, it had become harder to believe recently. He could see how happy Hayes was with Rikar, and he wanted the same. His being wary of strangers made it harder, but Rory wasn't a stranger, and Jessup's owl agreed. Rory was theirs. He was their mate, which meant he'd make them happy, but also that they needed to protect him.

They'd already failed that part of the job.

Jessup told himself he couldn't have helped Rory because he hadn't even known him, but now he did, and he'd make sure nothing ever happened to him again. That meant he had to be in Rory's life, though.

Could he do that?

Jessup was so fucking confused, and he didn't know how to untangle his feelings and thoughts.

Rory stared at Jessup for what felt like an eternity while Moore asked what was happening and Olga cackled. Jessup did his best to ignore them, and it was easier when Rory stuck his hand out.

"I'm Rory."

Jessup cleared his throat. "I know."

Rory didn't lower his hand, and Jessup could tell he wouldn't until Jessup did what he wanted, which clearly was to shake his hand. Jessup's fingers trembled when he raised his, but he grabbed Rory's hand and gave it a shake.

He couldn't let it go.

Rory's skin was soft, but his palm was a little clammy, as if he'd been nervous. He probably was, and Jessup understood because he felt he was about to jump out of his skin.

"I'm Jessup." Jessup's voice didn't sound like his. It was rougher, and he cleared his throat a few times.

"Thank you for saving me."

"It's my job."

Rory cocked his head. "Rikar mentioned something about that. Your job is to raid labs and save the people locked up inside them?"

"Pretty much."

"You should probably let go of the man," Moore suddenly said, reminding Jessup that he was still clutching Rory's hand.

He let go as if it had burned him, and to his surprise, Rory turned to glare at Moore. "What did you do that for?"

Moore looked confused. "Am I missing something? I thought that having Jessup hold your hand might make you feel awkward but that you were too afraid of asking him to let go."

"I'm not afraid of him."

Jessup breathed more easily. It was good to know his mate wasn't afraid of him, but that didn't solve his problem. What was he supposed to do with Rory?

"It would be understandable if you were."

Rory's glare deepened. "Are you afraid of your mate?"

Moore frowned. "Well, no."

"Then why should I be afraid of mine?"

In hindsight, telling everyone in the room that Jessup was his mate probably wasn't the smartest thing Rory could have done. He should have allowed them to talk about it alone, but part of him had been afraid that Jessup would refuse. For some reason, he seemed wary of being Rory's mate, and Rory supposed he hadn't wanted to give him the opportunity to say no.

Except in his own way, Jessup *was* saying no. He stared at Rory with horror, then ran out of the room. He didn't look back at Rory or anyone else in the room. No, he just barreled out, and when Rory moved to go after him, Rikar caught his arm.

Rory pulled, but Rikar didn't let go. When Rory turned to glare at him, he shook his head. "Let him go."

"I should apologize." Rory was hurt, but he could see he was in the wrong. "I shouldn't have announced that before we had time to talk."

"That's an understatement," Moore said.

Rory had briefly met Moore last night when he'd come to the house with a bunch of people he and the others had rescued from the lab. They'd been introduced, but they hadn't spent a lot of time together, and Rory found him intimidating. From what Rory had gathered, Moore was the leader of the group of people who rescued the prisoners from the labs. He was in charge of everyone, including Jessup. Rory couldn't afford to make an enemy out of him, so instead of snapping at him the way he wanted to, he swallowed, took a deep breath, and told himself to stay calm.

"I didn't mean to hurt him or to force him into anything. You have to understand how shocking it was for me to meet my mate in these circumstances, though. I'm already confused enough as it is. Meeting Jessup hasn't made things easier, but I really could use the support, and I thought he could give that to me." Rory looked at the door Jessup had left through. "Clearly, I was wrong."

Rikar cupped Rory's elbow and guided him toward the table. Rory flopped back into his chair, wrapped his fingers around his mug because he needed something to hold onto, and kept his gaze downward. He didn't know these people and didn't like feeling like they were judging him. He'd be the first to admit he'd done this the wrong way, but what did they expect? How would they have done it if they'd been in his place?

Rikar sat next to Rory and gently touched Rory's knee. "I don't think he was rejecting you."

"It sure looks like he did."

"He freaked out," another man said.

There had been so many introductions last night that Rory didn't remember this man's name. He didn't want to seem rude and ask, but he was curious, because he'd come in with Jessup.

Rikar nodded. "Leon is right. He's one of Jessup's best friends. He wouldn't lead you down the wrong path."

Rory eyed Leon. "Where will he lead me?"

Leon grinned and flopped at the table. "Hopefully, into Jessup's bed."

Moore slapped the back of Leon's head. "That's not what the bond between mates is about."

Leon scowled as he rubbed his head. "Not just, but you can't tell me you don't enjoy your time in bed with your mate."

Moore's eyes narrowed. "Don't you dare mention my mate."

"I won't, because he's a sweetheart. You get what I was trying to say, right?" he asked, turning to Rory.

Rory had no idea what was happening. "You want me and Jessup to end up together?"

Leon beamed. "Exactly. I'm one of his best friends, and I want him to be happy. Mates usually make people happy, which means the two of you need to get together."

"That's not going to be easy if he runs when he sees me."

Leon shrugged. "He only ran because you scared him to death." He hesitated, then leaned closer. "I'm going to tell you a few things about him. I probably shouldn't because it's his business and private, but I think it'll help you understand him better, and considering everything, you need that right now."

Rikar got to his feet, getting everyone's attention. "We can leave Leon and Rory here. Moore, Olga, why don't you come with me? We'll visit some of the other survivors."

Olga had been grinning the entire time, and she winked at Rory on her way out. Moore seemed more hesitant, but he clearly trusted Leon enough to leave him alone with Rory.

Rory hoped no one would regret that, including him.

Leon waited until everyone was out of the room. He poured himself a cup of coffee, and by the time he was done and sitting in front of Rory again, Rory felt like he was about to jump out of his skin.

"What did you want to tell me?" he asked.

"He's a loner. He always has been for as long as I've known him. We met after we were both freed from the labs, so while I do know something about his life before that, it's not much. He was alone when we met, and that has never changed. Most of us had a family who was looking for us the entire time we were kept prisoners. We went back once we left, and they were happy to get us back. Jessup didn't have that. I'm not sure what happened exactly, but he never visits his family and shuts down when anyone mentions it. He says he doesn't have anyone, and while that's hard to believe, I don't think he's lying. I believe something happened to make it so, and whatever that was, it still hurts him."

Rory thought about where he would be if he didn't have his family. They had to be worried sick and no doubt looking for him already, even though it had only been a couple of days since he'd been taken. "You're saying he's the kind of guy who pushes everyone away so they can't hurt him."

Leon shrugged. "I guess he is. Me and the others have managed to get through, but it wasn't easy. I think the fact that we all were in the labs helped, as well as all of us having special abilities now. It gives him a sense of family, but you don't share the same experiences."

Rory glared. "It doesn't mean we're not family or that we can't be."

"I never said that. I'm convinced that if he lets you in, you'll make him happy, and he deserves that. I want him to have it."

"But he won't make things easy on me."

"He doesn't make things easy on anyone, to be honest. We all know he's afraid of trusting people and getting hurt again, but you're his mate. You're not just some random guy, and while I'm sure that you'll eventually hurt him in one way or another, you'll never do it on purpose, and more importantly, you won't leave him behind."

That was one thing Rory could promise. "Never."

Leon nodded. "That's why I decided to talk to you. I want you to make Jessup happy, and that's not going to happen if you don't know what you're facing. So, now you do. You know he's going to push you away because he's terrified that if he opens up to you, you'll stomp on his heart and leave it broken. It won't be easy to break through his shield, but if there's one person who can, it's you."

Leon had a lot of faith in Rory, and Rory hoped he wouldn't disappoint him. More importantly, he hoped he wouldn't disappoint Jessup.

He didn't know what Jessup expected from a mate, but it was clear he thought Rory would hurt him. Rory wanted to show him that wouldn't be true, but to do so, he needed Jessup to allow him in. He didn't feel it would happen right now, but Rory was stubborn.

He and Jessup were supposed to be together. It was destiny, which meant it was Rory's right to pursue Jessup. He'd never force Jessup to do anything he didn't want, but he wouldn't know what Jessup wanted until they talked.

Rory sighed. He hadn't expected any of this to be easy, but he hadn't thought it would be so complicated. The fact that he'd been kidnapped made it worse, and he wasn't sure where to start when it came to dealing with all of it. He knew what he wanted, though, and what he was ready to do to get it.

He got to his feet. "I have to call my family."

Leon blinked at the sudden change in topic, but he nodded and reached into his pocket to take out a phone. "You can use my phone."

"Thank you."

"What will you tell them?"

Rory sucked in a breath. "That I met my mate and that I'm moving here."

Leon whistled. "You're not one to waste time."

"Not when something so important is at stake." Rory had an entire night to think about it, and like always when he made important decisions, he knew he wouldn't change his mind.

CHAPTER THREE

"What do we have?" Moore asked, looking around the room.

Jessup felt like he was back in school as he avoided looking at his leader. It was like he hadn't studied for his test. He hoped that if their eyes didn't lock, Moore wouldn't ask him questions.

Jessup had been surprised when Moore hadn't asked about what had happened with Rory. Jessup had expected everyone to want to know what was going on, but instead, they'd left him alone. Olga kept staring at him, and Leon looked like he wanted to say something a dozen times a day, but they weren't pushing, and Jessup was grateful. He also knew them well enough to be sure it wouldn't last much longer, unfortunately. He'd have to face what was happening, which was that he'd found his mate and had absolutely no clue what to do with him.

But for now, he had work to focus on. Yesterday, Moore and a few other members of their team had talked to the survivors and the healers who'd taken care of them. Today, they were having a meeting, like always after a raid. They gathered all their information, looked at what they had, and made decisions. Sometimes they planned more raids. Other times, they decided to leave it to the council and move on to something else. It depended on what they found, which was why it was important for them to talk.

"What about the three guys in the van?" Olga asked. "Who are they? Why were they there, following whose orders?"

Moore nodded at her. "We need answers to all these questions and more. Unfortunately, no one we talked to seems to be able to give us answers."

"I can somewhat help," Teddy said. "I had a bit of a chat with the guy when I shimmered him here. I was trying to make sure he didn't have more friends hiding around, but it was only the three of them."

And two had run away. That was a problem, and Jessup had no doubt they'd see them again. Whatever was happening wasn't good, but nothing ever was when it came to the labs.

"What did our prisoner tell you?" Moore asked, leaning forward.

Jessup was interested, too. He might not know what to do with Rory, but that didn't mean he didn't want to find out what had happened to him and whose ass he had to kick.

"Once he was done begging for his life, he turned to threats. Apparently, he thinks he's a hunter. There's a group of them active in the area who grab shifters and other paranormal creatures from the streets and take them to labs. It's how they earn a living. They sell us to these people and deliver us into their hands. They don't care what happens to us once we're in a cage. If I have to guess, I'd say they're actually happy we end up behind bars. That asshole certainly was eager to tell me that we deserve it because we're not human."

Moore pinched the bridge of his nose. "And here I thought that humans had finally gotten used to us after all these years."

"There are bigots everywhere, and there always will be."

Moore nodded curtly. "I agree. Unfortunately, the fact that these guys call themselves hunters means they're probably organized, at least in some ways."

"Enough to coordinate with the labs," Olga pointed out. "They found out about them even though they're a secret to the majority of the population, and they know what the scientists need. They have no problems providing them with people to experiment on, which means they have a way to identify us. They probably notice details we don't think to hide anymore, then spy on us for a while before taking us."

The thought made Jessup shudder. He could too easily imagine Rory going about his day, shopping at the grocery store, and the three guys from the other night staring at him from their van. The image that thought created in his mind was enough for him to want to rage, find the prisoner, and kick his ass.

"Is our prisoner talking now?" Moore asked. "We need to know more about these hunters, especially their numbers. Do we have to worry about them, or are they a small group we can wait to deal with?"

"He hasn't said anything," Hayes said with a grimace. "Rikar went over this morning, and the guy insulted him. He's clearly torn between being terrified of what we'll do to him and feeling like we're monsters and he's in the right."

"What about the three captured people in the van? Did they say anything that could help us?"

Jessup didn't miss the way Moore carefully avoided looking at him. He was grateful, but unfortunately, Moore was the only one who made that effort. Olga, Leon, and Hayes turned to Jessup as one, getting everyone's attention.

Jessup swallowed, glared at Leon, and got to his feet. Everyone was already staring anyway, and he had no intention of sticking around to answer questions. If they wanted to know what had happened, they needed to talk to Rory, not to him.

Jessup didn't say anything. He turned and headed for the door, ignoring Hayes hissing at him to stay. Moore didn't try to stop him, and as soon as he was out of the room, Jessup took a deep breath.

What the fuck was he doing? What was he *supposed* to do? He had no idea what people expected from him, and honestly, he wished someone would give him an order. Orders were easier to deal with than having to find out what to do by himself.

"Where do you think you're going?" Leon asked.

He'd followed Jessup out of the room—of course he had. He couldn't leave this alone, and Jessup regretted telling him that Rory was his mate. Leon wouldn't be sticking his nose where it didn't belong if he hadn't.

Jessup turned to glare at his friend. "Let it go, will you?"

Leon glared right back. He put his hands on his hips, and he might have looked intimidating if he hadn't been several inches shorter than Jessup. Jessup wasn't surprised he'd been the one who followed him. He and Hayes were just as close, but Hayes was nowhere near as confrontational. He'd give Jessup time to cool down and wrap his mind around what was bothering him. Leon, not so much. He already knew what was bothering Jessup.

"I won't," Leon declared. "If anything, because your mate doesn't deserve it. What the fuck are you doing, Jessup?"

"Do you think I know? Because if you do, you couldn't be more wrong. I have no clue about anything right now."

Jessup's expression softened just a bit. At the very least, he didn't look like he wanted to strangle Jessup anymore. "I can't say I know how that feels, but what you're doing is unfair. Do you know that Rory thought you were rejecting him yesterday? He freaked out when you left the room, and I had to sit him down and tell him about your family, or lack thereof."

A sense of panic gripped Jessup's chest. "You told him about my family?" He felt like he couldn't breathe, which didn't make sense. He had nothing to hide, even though he hated the fact that his family hadn't cared enough about him to look for him when he'd been taken.

Leon dropped his hands and took a step closer. "I didn't give him details because I don't have them. What did you think I could reveal? You've never told me or anyone else about your family. We just know they didn't look for you when you were taken and that you never went back."

"You don't need to know anything else."

"You're right. I don't. I only need to know that you don't want a relationship with them. It's the only thing I care about, but I wanted Rory to understand what he was up against. I might not know exactly what your family did to you, but I don't need to in order to see how much they hurt you. You've been keeping people at arm's length, and now, that includes your mate. That's not right. You should at least give him a chance, even if you eventually decide you don't want to be with him."

"I don't know what I want," Jessup whispered.

"I understand. You were shocked when you met Rory, and now you're not sure you can let him into your life. He'd understand if you told him more about your past. He seems like a nice guy, and since he's your mate, he has to be good for you, right?"

Because Rory was supposed to love Jessup. That was what mates were about.

The problem was that it was also what parents were about. They were supposed to protect their children, to worry about them, and to be there for them, not to abandon them when they were kidnapped and locked behind bars, experimented on, and turned into something that wasn't quite human—or shifter—anymore.

Rory liked making plans. He liked knowing what he was supposed to do that day, the next day, and even the entire week. He had a planner and scheduled everything he could, which helped him feel like he had his life under control.

He had nothing under control right now. His life was a mess, and he didn't know what to start with. His parents wanted him to go home, and he kinda wanted the same thing, but he needed to get used to the idea that this small town would be his home from now on. He was planning on moving but hadn't started anything to make that happen. He needed a new job, an apartment, and to talk to Rikar about moving, since he was the guy in charge.

He also needed to talk to Jessup.

That was where his mind snagged. It would make sense for him to talk to his mate before moving all the way here. What would happen if Jessup decided he didn't want anything to do with him? They'd both be uncomfortable because they lived in the same town, and it was tiny. Rory didn't want to give up his plans of moving, though. He belonged here, and he knew that in his bones. This was his home, whether or not Jessup was in his life.

And right now, he wasn't.

Rory sighed and pressed his forehead against the cool glass of the window. Staring at the trees outside his bedroom hadn't helped, but he hadn't expected it to. He just wasn't sure what to do, or rather, he knew what he needed to do but had no idea how to do it. His next step had to be talking to Jessup, but how was he supposed to do that when he couldn't get the man to stay still around him? He'd seen Jessup this morning, but his mate had taken one look at him and turned right around. Rory would have been offended if he hadn't known that Jessup was terrified of their bond, not of him.

In a way, it made sense. Rory hadn't expected to meet his mate, especially not in the situation they'd been in. Having someone like that in his life changed many things, and it came at a moment that was already confusing enough. Rory had been kidnapped. He'd lost his sense of safety, as well as his job. His life before wasn't his future, and he wasn't sure he'd ever feel safe again.

A knock on his bedroom door made Rory jerk away from the window. He stared at the door for a moment, against all odds hoping it was Jessup. Instead, when he went to open, it was to find Moore and Leon standing there.

"Hey," Leon said with a wide smile. "Sorry to bother you, but we'd like to ask you a few more questions if that's okay?"

"Of course." Rory wanted these people to catch the guys who'd kidnapped him, and he was ready to give them any information they needed to make that happen.

"A few others are waiting for us downstairs," Moore added.

He kept his distance from Rory as if he thought Rory was afraid of him. He might have been before because Moore was intimidating, but it was nothing next to what those assholes with the van had done to him. Rory was more afraid of humans at this point. No shifter had ever hurt him. Humans, on the other hand? They'd ruined his life.

"I can come downstairs," he confirmed. "Actually, it's probably a good idea if I leave this bedroom for a while. It's been hard to do that, but I need to."

Moore nodded as if he understood, and he probably did. Rory didn't know much about the people who'd rescued him, but he was aware of the fact that most of them had been in one of those horrible labs at one time or another. That included Moore, which was hard to believe because of how strong the man was, but strength had nothing to do with the fact that they'd been kidnapped.

Rory followed Leon and Moore downstairs. For some reason, Leon kept staring at him. It probably had something to do with Jessup, and thinking about him made Rory realize that he didn't know if his mate would be there. He wanted to ask, but he was also afraid of the answer. He wasn't quite sure which one he wished for, either.

"We already talked to Alma," Moore said as they walked into the living room. "She couldn't tell us much, unfortunately. She was kidnapped from a parking lot like you, stuck into that van, and that was that. They didn't answer when she tried to ask questions, which isn't surprising."

Rory nodded. "Unfortunately, I doubt there's anything else I can tell you." He looked around the room, not surprised to see that both Rikar and Olga were there. What did surprise him was seeing that Jessup was, too.

He was sitting on the couch, so tense that he looked like he might run away if Rory as much as looked his way. Rory had no idea what to make of the fact that he was present, but he hoped it was a good sign.

He needed it to be.

"Why don't you sit down?" Moore said, gesturing at the spot on the couch next to Jessup.

It would be interesting to see how Jessup reacted, so Rory obeyed without arguing. He also might have sat a bit closer to Jessup than strictly necessary, but he doubted anyone would blame him for that. If anything, Leon looked like he wanted to high-five him.

"Tell us what happened to you," Olga said, leaning forward.

"I was at the grocery store. I'm pretty sure I saw at least one of the guys who took me in the store, but I didn't give it much thought at the time. He was just a guy in the grocery store, you know? Anyway, I grabbed everything, checked out, went to my car, and opened the trunk. I remember putting one of the bags inside the trunk before I felt someone behind me. I started to turn, but whoever it was pulled a bag over my head. I freaked out and tried to fight him off, but he wasn't alone, and between the two of them, they dragged me away from my car. They pushed me into the van, and one of them tied my hands. He didn't take the bag off my head right away, but I could feel the van moving, so I knew we weren't at the grocery store anymore. I tried asking all three of them why they'd taken me, but they just grumbled something about me being a filthy animal or something like that."

Olga shook her head. "I don't understand humans."

"Most of them are okay people." Rory truly believed that even though he wasn't sure he could trust any of them at this point. "Some of them are assholes, but I suppose the same goes for shifters."

"Shifters have done horrific things to each other," Olga agreed. "But from what little we were able to find about the people who took you, they consider themselves hunters, and they're not hunting animals."

The realization felt heavy. "They hunt shifters."

Olga nodded. "And other supernatural creatures, but you get the idea. They take us off the streets, then hand us over to the scientists in the labs. We suspect that's how they finance their hunter business, plus it gives them a reason to hunt us." She snorted. "As if they need one."

So the labs paid for the kidnapped shifters, or maybe even *to* kidnap shifters. It wasn't a surprise, even though it made Rory feel less human. "I don't think it was the first time they did this. It felt too practiced."

Things were supposed to be different now, but that had been so for the past two decades. Rory had had high hopes when shifters came out to the world, but now, he wondered if they should have kept their existence a secret. He was sure some shifters had benefited from coming out to the humans, but from his point of view, many more had been hurt. Most humans didn't care about shifters and their existence, but they didn't stand up to the ones who did, and it made them as bad as these fucking hunters.

It would be a while before he could trust a human again.

Rory was strong. He'd come downstairs to talk to Moore and the others, and he was telling them everything he knew without hesitation. Jessup had no doubt he was freaking out, but he didn't allow it to show, even though no one would have blamed him. They knew what he'd gone through. They knew how it felt, how terrifying it was, which was why they were always careful with the survivors. They hadn't even considered talking to Benedict because of the state he was in. He might have been able to give them answers, but no one wanted to hurt him more than he already was. That was why Jessup had been hesitant when Moore had declared he wanted to talk to Rory again and why he'd decided to be here.

He might not know what to do with his mate, but his owl was sure of one thing—Rory was theirs to protect, even from Moore.

They talked to Rory for a while longer, but just like he'd explained in the beginning, he didn't have much to add. He hadn't been with the hunters for long, and while he was able to give them a few details, the only one who could give them better information was the hunter they were keeping prisoner.

And Jessup couldn't wait to talk to the guy.

"Rory, thank you," Moore said as he got to his feet. "What you went through is awful. You're welcome to talk to any of us if you need anything. We know what you're going through, and while some of us are still dealing with what happened to us, I can promise you that time makes things easier."

Rory smiled sweetly. "Thank you. I wouldn't be here if it weren't for you. You saved my life, and I'll always be grateful for that."

"It's our job."

"It's your job because you decided it would be. Me and the

other people you saved have a lot to be thankful for, and you should allow us to do so, at the very least."

Moore looked away. None of them did this because they wanted to be thanked. They did it because it was the right thing to do and because even though they could change into animals, they were human beings who didn't deserve to be in cages and turned into mutants.

"We're heading out to talk to the hunter we captured. If you want, we can let you know what we find out. It might help you get closure."

Rory's gaze flicked to Jessup. Maybe he wondered if Jessup would be going with Moore, and if he'd asked, the answer to that question would have been yes. Jessup wasn't going to miss this. He realized he needed to talk to Rory and that they had to make decisions, but his instincts were to protect his mate first and foremost. Once he was sure Rory wasn't in danger, they'd be able to sit down together.

Hopefully.

Rory nodded. "I'd like to know why they targeted me, at the very least. It gives me the creeps to think they might have been watching me, you know?" Rory shivered. "Maybe they even knew where I lived. I don't think I can ever go back to that apartment."

"We'll find a solution. You can stay here for as long as you need, as I'm sure Rikar told you. Don't worry about anything but getting better."

Rory nodded, but he wrapped his arms around himself. It was clear he didn't feel safe, and while Jessup wanted nothing more than to fold him in his arms and snarl at anyone who came too close, the best way to keep his mate safe was to find out why he'd been targeted and to make sure it couldn't happen again.

So when Moore left the room, Jessup was right behind him. No one tried to stop him, even though Leon glared. Jessup was focused on what was about to happen, and he followed Moore out of the house and through the village.

It was more like a small town by now, but it still had that small village feel. Everyone knew everyone, and it was a safe place for the survivors to heal and get their feet under themselves. They were completely safe here, even though several of them didn't seem to believe that yet. They would, in time.

"I don't like any of this," Moore muttered.

"We need to find out how they find the shifters."

Moore nodded. "It could be as simple as them using social media. A lot of shifters aren't as careful these days."

"It's not fair."

"It's not, but then when have humans been fair to shifters?"

He wasn't wrong, although Jessup had seen relationships between humans and shifters that worked, even without a mate bond. Unfortunately, the humans who were truly on their side weren't nearly enough, especially next to the ones who were against them.

"Do you want to talk about it?" Moore suddenly asked.

It took a moment for Jessup to understand what he was talking about. "Not really."

Moore nodded. "I won't push, but I want to remind you that I wasn't exactly happy when I found out Jolyn was my mate. I didn't know what to do about it, and I didn't believe I'd be any good for him. Sometimes, I still think that."

"There's no better man than you, especially for Jolyn."

Moore shrugged. "I know that, and you know you're it for Rory. Sometimes it's hard to convince yourself, though."

Jessup felt the same way. "I'm damaged. Emotionally, I mean, although I'm pretty sure I'm a train wreck in many ways. I have no idea if I can give him what he deserves, and the thought of hurting him makes me panic. It's easier to keep him away and keep safe from afar."

"I understand all of that, but do you think it's fair to him?

He's an adult, and even though he's been through hell, he knows what he's doing. He can make his own decisions, and you shouldn't take that away from him, especially after those hunters took everything from him. They didn't give him a choice."

And Jessup wasn't, either. It might not be in the same way, but it still hurt Rory, and it wasn't fair.

He swallowed, but his mouth was dry. "I promise I'm working on it." He was trying to convince himself that he deserved Rory, but he wasn't sure he'd be able to. Maybe that wasn't what he needed to commit himself to, though. Maybe just being there for Rory and attempting to be what he needed would be enough.

They finally reached the tiny cabin in the woods where they kept their prisoners. To be honest, the hunter was their first prisoner, but Rikar had insisted he be kept as far away from the town as possible. Jessup agreed. He didn't want Rory to feel threatened by this guy's proximity.

"How are we doing this?" he asked when they reached the door. "Good cop, bad cop?" He nodded at Davey, who stood by the door guarding it.

Everyone had agreed Jessup wouldn't be asked to do that, even though everyone else took a turn. Jessup suspected they thought they wouldn't find the hunter in one piece if Jessup was left alone with him.

Moore's grin was almost feral. "How about we're both bad cops?"

Jessup couldn't stop himself from grinning back. "I like that plan." And if it helped them get answers out of the hunter, all the better. He wouldn't hesitate to hurt the guy if it meant keeping Rory safe. After what the man had done, it was all he deserved, and Jessup would make sure he knew never to hurt a shifter again.

That was, if the guy had enough fingers left to hurt anyone.

Jessup wasn't normally so bloodthirsty, but this guy had hurt his mate, and he wouldn't stand for that. His owl wouldn't, either, and it was eager for the hunt. It wouldn't be a great one since the guy was tied up to a chair, but they could deal with it if it meant keeping their mate safe. That was all both of them wanted.

And maybe to shed a little blood.

Rory was a little lost, but he understood why Jessup had left this time. He wasn't running from him. He was doing his job, and Rory respected that, even though having Jessup leave him behind again hurt a bit. Thankfully, he didn't have to think about it for too long, because Leon stepped up next to him before he could go back to hide in his bedroom. "Hey, I'm having lunch with a friend. Do you want to come?"

Rory hadn't expected that. "Are you asking me because I'm Jessup's mate?"

"Well, yeah. Hayes and I are both close to Jessup, and we want to get to know you."

Rory wasn't offended. These guys didn't know him, yet they were willing to have a meal with him and include him in their lives because of who he was to Jessup. His first instinct was still to say no, but if he was going to move here, he needed to get to know people, especially Jessup's friends. "I'll come."

Leon looked like Rory had given him the moon. He beamed and quickly gestured to Hayes, who was talking to his mate by the living room door.

Rory was slowly learning names and who was with whom. It seemed that so far, in the group of people who'd rescued him, only a few of them had met their mates. Several were in relationships, though, and they felt like a big family. Eating lunch with Leon and Hayes would be almost like eating lunch with Jessup's brothers, and while that made Rory nervous, he was ready.

For lunch, at least.

Hayes gave Leon a thumbs up, turned to kiss his mate goodbye, then hurried toward Rory and Leon. Rory looked down at himself, relieved he hadn't stayed in his pajamas like he'd wanted. He wasn't wearing anything special, just jeans and a sweater, but he doubted they were going anywhere too posh for lunch.

"Let's go," Leon said, hooking his arm around Rory's. "The food at the diner is delicious. You'll want to eat there every day once you taste their food."

Rory doubted that. "I like cooking for myself."

Leon gasped dramatically. "Really? Because I swear, I can't even boil water without ruining the pot. Do you think you could teach me?"

Rory wasn't sure if Leon was asking because he actually wanted to learn or because he was trying to be friendly, but it didn't matter. "I guess it depends on why you're so bad at it."

"He gets distracted too easily," Hayes explained. "He puts the pot on the stove, then gets distracted by the TV, or a book, or a phone call. By the time he's done and back in the kitchen, it's a miracle if he hasn't set something on fire."

Leon didn't even look sorry. "I have many things to dedicate myself to," he said.

"As long as you don't hurt yourself. I'm pretty sure it's safer for everyone to keep you away from the stove, though."

The two of them bickered lightly as they walked down the street. Listening to them made Rory smile, and he could easily see himself becoming the third in their little group. Maybe fourth? He wasn't quite sure what kind of relationship Jessup had with these two, except that they were close. Maybe in a few weeks, there would be four of them walking down the street headed to lunch.

Rory's stomach churned at the thought of why Jessup wasn't with them. He was interrogating a prisoner, and while in theory, Rory wanted the guy to feel pain for what he'd done to him, Alma, and Benedict, in practice, it made him want to throw up. He didn't want to think about anyone being tortured. It didn't matter that this guy deserved it.

"So how are things going with Jessup?" Leon asked.

"They're not going."

"I talked to him, you know?"

Rory wasn't surprised. "What did you tell him?"

"That he needed to get his head out of his ass. I pointed out that these asshole hunters took every choice away from you and that he didn't have the right to do the same, that you're an adult, and that you need to know what's going on. I also mentioned that I told you about his family, and he kind of freaked out. That was probably not the best idea."

"I don't want him to be angry at me."

Hayes shook his head. "I don't think he is. But he's never told anyone about his family, and we all wonder why."

"He hasn't even told you?"

"No. We just know that his family didn't look for him when he vanished and that while he went back to them once after he was released, he never went again. I don't know what happened, and I don't think he'll ever tell anyone."

"Well, if he's going to tell someone, it has to be Rory, right?" Leon asked.

Rory wanted that. He wanted Jessup to trust him with his darkest secrets and the things that most mattered to him. He wanted Jessup to feel safe with him, to the point that he could tell him what his family had done to him.

Rory's family loved him, and he couldn't imagine what it was like to have a family who didn't care whether he was dead or alive. He wanted to fix things for Jessup, even though he realized how impossible it was. His own family would never become Jessup's, but maybe, they could still be part of his life.

Something told Rory that making that happen would be even more difficult than getting Jessup to open up to him.

"He keeps everyone away," he said.

Hayes nodded. "He's afraid that if he lets anyone in, they'll hurt him. I can't say I blame him."

"I'm not planning on hurting him."

"He'll realize that. He knows that his relationship with you will be different from the relationship he had with his family. You're his mate, and that's important. He wants to give you a chance because of that, but he's still terrified. I can't promise it'll work out, but I'll make sure he at least tries."

"As will I," Leon said.

He pulled Rory toward the door of the diner, and the three of them stepped in. The air smelled heavenly, and Rory's stomach growled, reminding him he hadn't been feeding it enough since he'd been released. He had a hard time eating anything, and when he did, it made him want to throw up. Hopefully, that wouldn't happen today because he wanted to relax, have fun, and act as if his life was entirely normal.

They slid into a booth, the fake red leather seat crackling under Rory's ass. The place had seen better days, but everything looked clean enough and was kind of cute.

"Pretty much everything is good here," Leon said as he snatched one of the menus and slid it toward Rory.

It was plasticized, the surface slightly yellow and sticky. Rory didn't dare touch it, but he leaned over it. He didn't know if he'd be able to eat, but he was certainly going to try.

"You know what you should do?" Hayes suddenly asked.

"What?" Hopefully, he was about to suggest what Rory should get for lunch.

But Hayes's smile told Rory he had something entirely different in mind. "You should woo Jessup."

Rory blinked, trying to get an image of how that would work. "He'd have to stop avoiding me first."

"He will eventually. I mean, he didn't run out of the room during the meeting today."

Rory supposed that was a good sign. "So—what? I should ask him out on a date?"

"Yeah. He needs to get to know you just like we are. We can give you tips about his favorite stuff, like food and whatever, and you can use that knowledge to make him fall for you. Then, once he's in love, he'll realize he can't live without you, and you'll be able to bond."

He made it sound simple, and Rory wanted that.

He wasn't afraid of working hard to get Jessup. He had his own hang-ups, although most of them were recent—as in, he had them because he'd been kidnapped. Jessup was different, yet at the same time, his problems came from what had happened to him in the labs. They were more similar than Jessup allowed himself to see, and Rory hoped it would help them connect at some level. It wasn't the best thing since it wasn't exactly a time in his life he wanted to think about, but maybe they needed to face their pain to heal.

What had happened to Jessup had hurt him in ways Rory could only imagine. Jessup had been avoiding it, but maybe that wasn't the answer. Maybe the answer was to face his past with Rory standing by his side.

CHAPTER FOUR

"Hey, Jessup?"

Jessup looked up at Hansen, who stood at the living room door. "Yes?"

"There's someone at the door for you."

Jessup blinked. "Who?"

Hansen shrugged. "One of the guys we rescued from the last lab."

It had to be Rory. There was no other explanation. No one else would come to visit Jessup, especially at home. Why was Rory here, though? They hadn't seen each other since the meeting the other day, but Jessup had been trying to find a way to reach out to him. He felt lost. He had no idea how to behave and was terrified of doing or saying the wrong thing. What would happen if he did? He didn't want to send Rory running, but he also wasn't sure he could push himself out of his comfort zone, even for his mate.

It looked like he could stop thinking about a way to meet Rory because Rory was here.

He swallowed and got to his feet. "I'll be right there."

Hansen nodded and left Jessup alone. That was good, because Jessup needed a moment, and he used it to pace the living room and tell himself that everything would be all right.

Everything had to be all right. Rory wasn't just a guy. He was Jessup's mate, and that meant something, both to Jessup and to him. If Rory didn't care, he wouldn't be here, trying to talk to Jessup.

There was no way to know how things would end up

between them, but Jessup could have hope. Rory seemed nice enough, and Jessup had promised he'd give him at least a chance. He owed it to him, and just maybe, he owed it to himself. His family had hurt him in the past, but that didn't mean Rory would hurt him now or in the future. The only way to find out if they could be happy together was to talk to Rory, though, and while Jessup wasn't ready, it looked like he wouldn't have a choice.

He stopped pacing, squared his shoulders, and strode toward the living room door. He didn't allow himself to stop, mostly because he knew that if he did, he'd run the other way. He was a coward when it came to protecting his heart. He'd run into a lab without hesitation, but this? It was absolutely petrifying.

The front door was open, but Hansen was nowhere to be seen. The only person there was Rory, who shuffled his feet on the porch, looking around as he did so. His eyes widened when he noticed Jessup, but he schooled his expression as if he was afraid Jessup would freak out if he appeared happy to see him.

Jessup was happy to see Rory. It was confusing because they didn't know each other, but the pull toward his mate was strong. The bond didn't care how hesitant Jessup was. His owl didn't, either. Both just wanted Jessup to stop being an asshole and accept Rory, and while Jessup wasn't sure he could do so right away, he could certainly try or, at the very least, give Rory a chance.

"Hi," Rory said, giving a little wave. For some reason, he glared at his hand and quickly pushed it into his pocket.

Maybe he thought he was ridiculous, but Jessup found it sweet. "Hi," he said, coming to a stop in front of Rory. "Do you want to come in?"

Rory cleared his throat, then shuffled his feet again. He was clearly nervous, which was entirely understandable. Rory didn't know how Jessup would take his visit, and to be honest, Jessup wasn't sure, either. If anyone had asked him what he'd do if Rory knocked on his door, he'd have told them he'd run away and hide. Instead, he was here, facing his mate.

Well, mostly ready.

Rory shook his head. "Actually, I'm here to take you on a date."

Jessup blinked, certain he'd misunderstood. There was no way he could have misunderstood those words, though. "A date?"

Rory leaned sideways and reached for something on the bench by the door. The bench was always full of blankets, coats, and various articles of clothing the mutants who lived here left there before and after they shifted. There were also boots and shoes under the bench, so it was a bit of a mess.

But Rory didn't offer Jessup a coat. Instead, he brought up a bunch of flowers that left Jessup staring at him once again.

Rory looked like he wasn't quite sure what to do, but he held out the red roses. "I wasn't sure what you liked, so I went with a classic."

Jessup stared because what else could he do? "I don't think anyone's ever bought me flowers."

Rory grinned, and it was a good look on him. "I can be the first."

Jessup took the flowers and brought them to his nose. They smelled almost as good as Rory, and the thought made Jessup smile wider. He hadn't expected this from his mate, and he wasn't quite sure how to react, but it was a nice gesture that made him feel cared for. He didn't know if that was what Rory had intended, but it was what Jessup needed.

The people who should have cared for him hadn't. It was a wound he'd always carry, but maybe it was time to allow it to heal. He could give Rory a chance, even though it was terrifying.

Jessup looked Rory up and down. Knowing he wanted to take him on a date explained why he looked so nice tonight. He wore dark jeans and a button-down shirt under his jacket. The clothes were clearly new, although that had more to do with the fact that Rory had survived the lab and was staying here temporarily rather than because he wanted to make a good impression. It didn't matter, because Jessup found him adorable whether he was wearing new clothes or a dirty and torn t-shirt like the night they'd met. He doubted Rory would like it if he admitted that, though. "You look good."

Rory blinked, then blushed. "Thank you. I know we didn't talk about this, so it's a surprise, but I'd love to take you on a date."

He'd already said that, and if he was repeating himself, he was clearly nervous. Jessup understood because he was nervous as hell, too. He didn't know what to expect from a date with his mate, but he was about to find out. There was no way he was rejecting Rory, especially when Rory was so nervous and probably expected him to. Jessup didn't blame him, considering the way he'd behaved these past few days, but it was time to stop running and being an idiot.

Jessup hadn't made decisions yet when it came to his mate. The thought of giving Rory his heart only to have Rory hurt him was scary enough to make him want to stay away, but it wasn't fair to Rory. His mate had never done anything to hurt Jessup, and Jessup shouldn't treat Rory as if he had. Rory wasn't his parents and his siblings. He wasn't about to abandon Jessup.

Jessup had to believe that.

He nodded. "And I'd love to go on a date with you. Give me a few minutes. I'll be right out."

Rory beamed. "I'm not going anywhere."

He really wasn't, was he? From the first time they met, Rory seemed to have known what he wanted, and that was a chance to be in Jessup's life. Even before they'd spoken, he hadn't hesitated, and Jessup was in awe of that. Rory knew what he wanted, and he wasn't afraid of it. Maybe he could give Jessup some courage, or maybe Jessup needed to stop thinking that Rory would hurt him. Rory wasn't just a guy. He was Jessup's mate, and that meant everything.

Jessup quickly washed up, put on clean jeans and a shirt, then grabbed his jacket. He felt jittery, but he knew everything would be okay.

It had to be.

By the time he was ready and at the front door again, Rory looked about to jump out of his skin. Still, he grinned when he saw Jessup, then stepped to the side to allow him to get to the porch. Jessup hesitated for only a moment. They were doing this, no matter how scared he was. It was just a date, not a proposal, and he owed it to Rory.

And to himself.

Rory didn't think he'd ever been so nervous. Scared, yes, but not nervous, and he wasn't quite sure how to behave. He tried to think about his past first dates, but they couldn't compare. The guys he'd dated had been nice, but they hadn't been his mate. He only had one of those, and that man was walking next to him on the sidewalk as if they did this every day.

It was terrifying.

"So what did you have in mind?" Jessup asked.

Rory swallowed. He realized how lucky he was that Hayes and Leon had helped him organize this. For one, they'd been able to tell him all the places in town where he could take Jessup. Rory wanted this to be special, but he also wanted Jessup to feel at ease. It would be no use for both of them to be uncomfortable, especially when Jessup was still hesitant about all of this. Rory needed his mate to give him a chance.

Once that happened, he was sure he could get Jessup to see they belonged together.

"Well, it wasn't easy to choose," he explained. "As you know, I'm not from around here, so I don't know the town well. I also don't know you, which didn't help."

Jessup nodded. "I won't be angry even if we do something I don't like."

"But I don't want you to do something you don't like."

Jessup smiled softly. "Let's see what you organized, all right?"

Rory swallowed. He had a plan, and he needed to stick to it. "I thought we could take a walk. The evening is nice, and it's a bit early for dinner. We can walk and talk, get to know each other." It was nothing special, but it felt important that they do that.

Thankfully, Jessup seemed to agree because he nodded and continued walking down the sidewalk.

The town was tiny, but it was growing. Shops that appeared brand-new lined the main street, and Rory and Jessup slowly walked past them. Rory used the distraction to take a moment to gather his thoughts. They were supposed to get to know each other, which meant one of them needed to start talking. Something told him that wouldn't be Jessup, which meant he had to make an effort.

"I called my family," he started. Then, he realized it was probably the worst topic of conversation he could have selected. He glanced at Jessup in horror, wondering if his mate was ready to run down the street trying to escape, but Jessup just nodded and smiled.

"Tell me about them," he said.

Rory didn't know what to make of that request, but he nodded. "If you're sure."

"I wouldn't ask if I wasn't."

That was probably true, and even if it wasn't, Rory had to

trust his mate to know what he wanted and, more importantly, what he needed. If Jessup didn't want him to talk about his family, he'd let him know.

"Well, they were happy to find out I was fine. They were freaking out, even though I was only gone for two days."

"I suppose that not knowing where your son is for two days is scary," Jessup said as if the words didn't have a deeper meaning.

Rory was dying to find out what Jessup's family had done to him. He wasn't sure Jessup would ever give him details, but what he did know of the situation made him want to rage. Jessup's family hadn't looked for him, even though he'd been gone much longer than two days. Rory could only imagine how that would have felt. He'd cried on the phone with his mom because he'd been so sure he'd never see her again, and she'd been terrified something had happened to him.

Rory cleared his throat. "It was scary, both for her and for me. She asked me to come home, but I told her I had something to do here."

"Does that something to do involve me?"

"You know it does."

Jessup hesitated. "I don't want to keep you away from your family."

"You're not."

"Yet you're here because of me."

"I'm here because I want to be. I already told her I was moving."

Jessup stumbled, and Rory reached for him on instinct. He grabbed Jessup's hand, and Jessup turned wide eyes to him. "You're moving?"

"I am. I like this place, and it's where you are."

"But what if I can't give you what you need? What if things don't work out between us?"

Rory wasn't surprised that Jessup's mind had gone straight

to the worst-case scenario. "But what if things *do* work between us? What if you give me everything I've ever wanted and make me happier than I've ever been? I know part of your past, so I can understand why you don't want to consider that possibility, but it's there, and I think it's stronger than the possibility that we'll fuck everything up. You're not just a guy. Being your mate means something, and I want things to work between us."

"I want that, too, but I don't know how to make it happen."

Rory was still holding Jessup's hand, and he squeezed it as he gave him what he hoped was a reassuring smile. "Maybe we can find out together?"

Jessup stared at him for so long that Rory thought his answer would be no and that maybe he was trying to find a nice way to let Rory down. To his surprise and relief, Jessup smiled at him. "All right. Let's try this. I can't promise I won't fuck it up, though."

"I don't need you to make promises you can't keep. I just need you to give me and us a chance."

"I will."

That was all Rory needed. He pulled Jessup along and continued talking about his family because it was a safe topic of conversation. They slowly walked down the sidewalk as Rory described growing up with his parents and his siblings. He carefully avoided talking about his shifted form, even though Jessup had to be able to smell that he was a shifter. Rory wasn't quite sure when he'd be ready to talk about that, but he didn't want to scare Jessup, and usually, people tended to stay away when he was in his shifted form.

The problems started when they walked past the park. A group of teenagers was hanging around, some of them in their human form, a few in their shifted form. The bunny cuddling on their friend's lap was adorable, and Rory wasn't the only one to think that because Jessup turned to him. "I haven't asked what kind of animal you shift into."

"I know."

Jessup arched a brow. "You're hiding something."

He sounded playful, so Rory wasn't too afraid, at least not about keeping this a secret. He *was* afraid that Jessup would freak out, though. "What kind of shifter are you?"

"I'm an owl."

"I like owls." They were normal, and people didn't run away from them.

"And you are?"

Rory sighed. "You're not going to let this go, are you?"

"I can if you don't feel comfortable, but I don't understand why you don't want me to know what you can shift into. I already know you're a shifter."

"I just don't want to weird you out. It was complicated enough to get you to agree to come on this date. I don't want to ruin it."

"I don't see how you could ruin it by telling me what kind of animal you shift into."

Rory pulled Jessup toward the deeper part of the park. The park was small, but it was open to the woods in which the small town had been built. It would give Rory enough privacy to be able to shift and show Jessup what the problem was. It was also close enough to tell him that Rory would be able to go back home if Jessup abandoned him. "My shifted form is unusual, and most people are weirded out, at the very least," he explained.

"Weirded out? I understand if you don't want to tell me, but I know many different kinds of shifters. If you want to see an unusual animal, you should ask Moore to shift for you."

"Yeah? What does he shift into?"

"A shoebill stork."

"Really? Those are the massive ones that sound like some-one's shooting at you, right?"

"That's the one. Is your shifted form as weird as that?"

"Yeah. I want to show you."

"You don't have to if you're not comfortable with it."

But Rory wanted to get this out of the way. He might as well since Jessup already knew something was up, and besides, he missed shifting. He tried not to do it too often, and it was easy to ignore that part of him when he focused on work and lived surrounded by humans. Here, though, no one would blink at him shifting or even wandering around town in his animal form. Most people who lived here were shifters or other supernatural creatures, and for them, it was normal.

Rory looked around. "I want to shift and show you."

"Then we can do that. How about we play around for a bit? It's been a while since I stretched my wings."

Rory swallowed. If he wanted Jessup to trust him, he needed to trust Jessup. "Let's do it." It hadn't been part of the plan, but this felt spontaneous. Terrifying, too, but this was what Rory and Jessup needed to get to know each other.

Jessup was curious. He didn't know what to expect from Rory's shifted form, but Rory wasn't comfortable with it. Was it that weird that he'd had people reject him over it before? Jessup wouldn't be surprised some humans had been assholes that way. Some of them were weird, and while they liked *normal* shifters, as they called them, anything out of the ordinary was rejected. Was that what had happened to Rory? And how out of the ordinary was he?

Jessup was about to find out. He'd shift, too, but first, he wanted to see Rory and reassure him that he didn't care even if he shifted into a purple cow.

But if that *was* what he shifted into, Jessup might ask him if purple cows made purple milk, just to make him smile.

Rory carefully avoided looking at Jessup as he stripped,

and Jessup kept his gaze away because they weren't there yet. For the first time, though, the thought of spending time with his mate didn't scare him. He hadn't realized Rory was as nervous as he was about this, but maybe he should have. They were mates, and the bond was as important to Rory as it was to Jessup.

"I'm shifting," Rory warned.

Jessup waited a moment longer to give Rory enough time to do so. Then, he finally allowed himself to look up.

His gaze crossed with Rory's, and it took a moment to wrap his mind around what he was seeing. He wasn't quite sure what Rory was, but he seemed to be some kind of deer. He had two horns that shot up straight from his head, not very long but big enough to hurt if he stabbed someone with them. His little furry ears twitched, and his dark eyes stared at Jessup.

The strange part was Rory's nose. Jessup had never seen anything like that. It was as if someone had elongated it. It dropped in front of Rory's mouth, making his muzzle look extremely long. That didn't make him ugly or scary, although Jessup could understand why some people might have felt that way.

He took a step forward, careful in case Rory wanted to run. Rory stayed where he was, though, standing proud. His fur was gray, mostly light, with some darker spots on his cheeks, and the light color made him highly visible even in the darkness.

Jessup held up his hand as if he was in front of a scared animal. Rory wasn't an animal, but he *was* scared. Clearly, he'd been rejected often enough that he'd been planning on keeping this side of himself away from Jessup for as long as he could. Jessup was glad they'd gotten over that hurdle already. He didn't want Rory to feel he needed to hide anything from him, but especially not this.

"Can I touch you?" he asked.

As an answer, Rory butted his forehead against Jessup's hand. It made Jessup smile, and he gently touched his fingertips to Rory's forehead, right between his horns. Rory moved closer, bumping his body against Jessup's legs. He was big enough to knock Jessup back, and the look of terror in his eyes when he realized what he'd done was enough for Jessup to want to strangle whoever had hurt him in the past.

"You were right when you said your shifted form is unusual," Jessup said as he rubbed Rory's soft fur. "I don't think I've ever seen the animal you turn into, but while it's odd, it doesn't mean it's ugly or anything like that. I quite like it, to be honest. I'm just a normal boring owl."

Rory huffed and pushed harder into Jessup's touch. Jessup obliged, stroking his fur and scratching under his chin. Rory glared at him, but he seemed to enjoy it, so Jessup continued.

"You'll have to tell me what kind of animal you are when you shift back because I'm curious."

Rory nodded, then, to Jessup's surprise, pushed his hand away. Jessup wondered if they were already done, but Rory didn't shift back. Instead, he continued staring at Jessup with his black eyes, clearly waiting for something.

It didn't take a genius to understand what he wanted. "You want me to shift?" Jessup asked to be sure.

Rory nodded. Jessup supposed it was only fair that he shifted, too. He didn't have the same hang-ups Rory clearly had when it came to shifting, so it wasn't a problem for him. As he'd explained, he was just a boring brown owl, nothing Rory hadn't seen before. Jessup was fine with that. He didn't need to be special, especially with his mind control ability.

Since Rory wanted to see him, he quickly stripped. He left his clothes with Rory's, then shifted, eager to stretch his wings. It had been too long because when they raided the labs, they needed strong shifters, not an owl. Jessup was useful because of his mutant ability, not because he was an owl shifter, and that was fine with him. He'd made his peace with it, even though he didn't like the fact that the labs had done something good. He wouldn't be able to rescue the survivors if it weren't for what the scientists had done to him, but that didn't mean he hated them any less.

He'd still set them on fire if he met them again.

As soon as he was naked, Jessup shifted. He was pretty sure that Rory was scowling at him, maybe because he'd hoped to get a peek at Jessup's naked body. Jessup wanted to tell him there would be time for that later, but he didn't dare, and once he was in his owl form, he couldn't speak anyway.

He stretched out his wings, chirping in pleasure at the feeling of the cool night breeze on his feathers. He wanted to fly, but first, he had something to do.

Jessup turned his attention to his mate. Rory stood there, and for a moment, nothing happened. They just stared at each other. This was another way to get to know each other, and Jessup enjoyed it. In his owl form, he couldn't say something stupid that would send Rory running. He could let the fear go, at least for a little while, and focus on having fun. That was what dates were about, wasn't it? Rory wanted to get to know him, but he also wanted to have fun with him, and Jessup was finally ready to let go.

Rory stepped closer and bumped his nose against Jessup's head. He was bigger than Jessup, and Jessup stumbled back, then glared at him. Rory's chest shook, and Jessup was pretty sure it was in laughter. He snapped his beak at Rory's nose, but Rory didn't seem intimidated. He took a step back, then looked up at the sky. They couldn't speak in this form, but they didn't need to because Jessup got the message.

He extended his wings again and took to the sky.

It felt good to have the wind under his wings again after so long. He circled over Rory for a moment, then cried out and headed deeper into the forest. He wasn't planning on going far, but his chest tightened when he looked down and saw Rory running after him between the trees. Rory wouldn't leave Jessup on his own. He was there for Jessup.

That was when Jessup finally let go.

He was still afraid. He doubted that would vanish anytime soon, but he could deal with it. If it meant having Rory in his life, he'd even go to the therapist Moore had hinted at several times.

Jessup wanted this to work. He wanted to let go of the past and the pain his family had caused and focus on the future. He wanted to trust Rory with his entire self and with his heart.

Rory hadn't known how Jessup would react to his shifted form. Some people liked it, but most of them, especially humans, were weirded out and gave him a wide berth. They didn't know what to make of it, but Jessup had taken it in stride. Rory doubted Jessup had ever seen a Saiga antelope before, but he hadn't seemed scared, and even now that he was flying away from Rory, he made sure to include him in the fun.

Jessup flew ahead, going up and down, circling around Rory as Rory ran. It was odd to play like this, but it had been too long since Rory had allowed himself to do it. It hadn't been easy because he'd lived in the city, and the fact that he wanted to hide his animal made it even more complicated.

But here, he didn't have to hide. Jessup accepted him, and Rory had no doubt that everyone else would, too. They'd probably be curious about him in the beginning and have questions, but they wouldn't care what he looked like in his shifted form.

Almost everyone who lived in this small town was part of the supernatural community. A lot of people were part of

Rikar's original tribe, which meant they were Nix. The others were a mix of the survivors who'd been rescued over the years and Jessup's people, and while a few were human, like Hayes, they might as well be part of the supernatural community. If Rory moved here, he'd never have to hide again, and that was enough to make him want to do just that. Jessup living here was the biggest incentive, but not the only one.

When Rory had told his mother what he was planning, she'd been worried, even after he'd explained he'd met his mate and wanted to be close to him. She'd been afraid he was going too fast and that he'd regret it, but he wasn't doing this only because he wanted to be with Jessup.

Okay, maybe in the beginning, that was why he'd decided to do it. He'd wanted to have a chance to be with Jessup, and that would be easier if he lived here. After spending a few days in this town, though, Rory could say he'd never felt more at home except in the house where he'd grown up. He belonged here, in the middle of these people who'd survived hell. Even though he'd been kidnapped, what he'd lived through wasn't anywhere as horrifying as some of the stories he'd heard. He realized how lucky he was and wanted to be part of this special place.

He hoped he'd be allowed to.

Rikar had already told him he was welcome to move into town and stay for as long as he wanted. He offered that option to every person they rescued from the labs, and while technically, Rory hadn't been *in* the lab, he'd still been rescued. This was his chance to live his life the way he wanted to, to be with his mate and maybe, build a family and become part of a supernatural community. He didn't have to stay in a small apartment with humans living all around him anymore. He didn't have to avoid shifting. Here, he'd be able to be himself, which was all he'd ever wanted.

He ran until he was out of breath. Jessup was still going,

but he realized Rory wasn't behind him anymore after a moment and turned back. Rory tilted his head toward the spot where they'd left their clothes, and Jessup seemed to understand what he was saying. Rory ran, but Jessup had already shifted back when he reached the spot. Rory glared at him because he'd wanted to take a good look at what his mate was hiding under his clothes, which Jessup seemed to find amusing because he grinned at him with the widest smile Rory had ever seen on his lips.

"You'll have the opportunity to see me naked eventually. I'm starving, though, and I don't know what you have planned for the rest of the date, but if it's okay with you, we could go to the diner."

Rory had been planning that, so he nodded eagerly and shifted back.

The spring air was cool on his human skin, and he understood better why Jessup had dressed right away. He did the same, shivering a few times as he slipped on his jeans, shirt, and jacket.

Once he was dressed, he turned to Jessup. He was a bit nervous again and wanted to know what Jessup thought of his shifted form. He doubted he'd have to ask. His hesitation was obvious, and Jessup was observant.

"What kind of animal do you turn into?" Jessup asked.

"It's a kind of antelope."

"Oh, I can see that. I thought you might be some kind of deer, but antelope makes sense."

Rory arched a brow. "You know a lot about antelopes?"

Jessup looked away, a small smile playing on his lips. "I like watching nature documentaries."

Rory laughed and hooked his arm around Jessup's. "Yeah? You can tell me about those documentaries as we walk to the diner. I'm hungry, too."

Jessup guided Rory out of the forest and toward one of the

paths. Rory went, happy even though this wasn't what he'd planned. But his biggest secret was out of the way, and Jessup had been welcoming of it. He wasn't afraid or weirded out. He accepted Rory just the way he was, which wasn't something Rory had expected.

But he loved it.

"Can I ask you why your nose is the way it is?" Jessup asked as they walked.

Rory thought about being a smart ass and asking Jessup why his wings were the way they were, but there was only curiosity in Jessup's tone. He wanted to know more about Rory and his animal form, and Rory wanted him to know. "I looked into it and found out it's to warm up cold winter air but also to filter out dust. Or at least, that's what people assume. There's no guarantee they're right."

"I think it's cute."

Rory laughed. "Really?" That wasn't what Rory would have called it. His antelope nose looked like two short elephant trunks side by side.

"Really. Don't get me wrong, I like bear and lion shifters as much as most humans seem to, but they're a dime a dozen. Give me unusual shifters all day, and I'll be happy."

Rory leaned closer. "Is that your kink? Seducing unusual shifters?"

Jessup hesitated, then freed his arm from Rory's hold. For a moment, Rory thought he'd fucked up, but Jessup didn't push him away. Instead, he wrapped his arm around Rory's shoulders and dragged him closer. He even kissed the top of Rory's head, which startled Rory as much as it pleased him.

"Not a kink. I'm interested in nature and know a lot about lions and bears. About your kind of antelope, though? I know next to nothing, and it's going to be interesting researching it."

So Jessup wasn't only accepting of Rory's shifted form, but

he was welcoming it. He wanted to learn more about it, and that touched Rory in a way he hadn't expected.

Rory's family had always accepted him, of course. His father was an antelope, as was his sister, while his mother and brother were wolf shifters. To them, Rory's shifted form was normal. Rory hadn't understood that wasn't the case until he'd shifted to play with his friends as a kid, and they'd made fun of him for his nose. Over the years, he'd become more careful about who he shifted in front of, but he wouldn't have to do so in front of Jessup or anyone in town. He was welcome here. He could be himself, and he didn't need to be afraid of how people would react.

"Thank you," Jessup said.

They were at the edge of the park, and they'd be back into town proper with only a few steps. Rory was hungry, but at the same time, he didn't want this moment with Jessup to end.

He turned to look up at Jessup. "What are you thanking me for?"

"For trusting me with something clearly important to you. I can tell it was hard, so I'm glad you trusted me enough to show me your antelope."

"You're my mate. If there's anyone I knew I could trust with this, it's you, and I'm glad I did."

"You're safe with me."

And Rory believed that.

He decided to take a chance and leaned closer to Jessup. Jessup's eyes widened, but he didn't move back, not even when Rory hooked an arm around his neck and pulled him down. Rory could see him holding his breath, but that wouldn't be a problem for too long.

Rory brushed their lips together, giving Jessup the time to make up his mind about what he wanted. When Jessup's hands landed on Rory's hips and he pulled him closer, Rory knew Jessup wouldn't push him away. He wanted this as much as Rory did.

So Rory kissed him.

It was slow, sweet, and gentle, and while it would be easy to deepen the kiss, Rory kept it that way. They didn't need to make out. This was not only their first kiss but also a way for him to tell Jessup how grateful he was that Jessup was accepting him so easily. He wanted Jessup to know how important this was to him, and he thought Jessup understood. Their lips moved against each other, their bodies pressed together, and once again, Rory could feel the certainty down to his bones.

He was home.

CHAPTER FIVE

It was time for another chat with Frank. The hunter wouldn't be happy to see Jessup, but Jessup didn't care. He wanted answers, and Frank hadn't given him and Moore much the first time they'd talked to him. Moore was convinced it was because Frank was a low-level hunter and that he didn't know anything, but Jessup wanted to be sure, especially now that things were going well with Rory.

They still needed to talk. They were both aware of that, and eventually, they'd do it. Jessup wanted to enjoy the time they spent together right now, though. They were getting to know each other, discovering what made the other smile, and he didn't want to ruin that with relationship talk. Besides, in the end, did they really need to talk about their relationship? They were mates, and it meant something for both of them. What was happening and all the changes in their lives was a lot, and Jessup wasn't in a hurry to talk things out and make decisions about the future. For now, he was fine dating Rory.

And beating up hunters.

Jessup suspected that would become part of the mission soon. Until now, they'd focused on the labs because they didn't want anyone else to get hurt, and that was what the hunters did. They hurt people without hesitation. They considered shifters nothing more than animals, but Jessup suspected that even if they'd considered shifters humans, they wouldn't have cared. These people were cruel and didn't care one bit about who they had to kill to make sure they became rich and powerful.

Well, Jessup had a surprise for them. They'd played with his DNA and turned him into something more in their attempt to create a super soldier, and that was going to bite them in the ass. Their own creations were rebelling against them, and they were stronger than they ever had been before.

"I'm still not sure this is a good idea," Hayes said, nervously looking around as if he expected his mate to jump up from behind a bush.

Jessup eyed him sideways as they continued walking down the sidewalk. "You don't have to come with me."

"You're going to get yourself in trouble if I let you do this alone. Moore said you almost killed the guy the last time you talked to him."

"I didn't almost kill him. I just poked him a little."

"With a knife in the guts. You could have killed him."

Jessup cracked his knuckles. "As long as he tells me what I want to know, I promise I won't poke him too hard this time."

Hayes didn't look convinced. "Considering your relationship with Rory, you should leave the interrogation to someone else."

"I'm not doing that."

"I was afraid you'd say that, which is why I'm coming with you."

But Hayes didn't have it in him to hurt people. Yes, he was one of the mutants, and he'd been on several raids, but he wasn't a killer.

To be fair, Jessup doubted any of them had been before. Even he had been just a normal person, living his life, going to work, and doing his best to be happy. What they'd done to him in that lab had hardened him, and he didn't feel remorse for killing scientists and the guards who worked for them. He probably should, but after what they'd done, he considered them nothing more than monsters, and he didn't regret killing monsters. It was the only way to make sure they could never hurt anyone else.

But Hayes was soft. Maybe it was because he was human, or maybe because the ability he'd been given wasn't offensive. Jessup didn't care either way, and he liked his friend the way he was. He didn't want Hayes to become a killer. He wanted Hayes to continue smiling, build a life with his mate, and be happy.

Jessup hadn't thought he could have that, but he'd been cheering for Hayes since he'd met Rikar. Now, it was his turn, and since his first date with Rory, he couldn't wait to see what would happen next between them.

Hopefully, a lot.

They finally reached the shed where Frank was kept prisoner. This time, it was Teddy who stood in front of it, guarding the hunter. He was playing with his phone, but he looked up when he heard them and slipped it into his pocket. He cocked his head, his gaze jumping from Hayes to Jessup. "Moore texted me to warn me you were coming," he said.

Jessup nodded. "I just want to talk to the hunter again."

"I'll come with you."

Hayes made a sound of protest. "That's my job. It's why I came here in the first place."

"You can stay outside and stand guard, or even better, go home to Rikar."

Clearly, Jessup wasn't the only one trying to shield Hayes from the nastiness of the situation.

Hayes rolled his eyes. "I know what the two of you are doing, and while I'm touched, you don't have to do it. I've seen blood. I've seen people tortured and wounded. I've even seen people die." He cleared his throat, his expression serious. "I might not have the guts to kill someone myself, but I was in one of those labs, too. I've seen what the scientists could do and what they did do. I even lived it on my skin, and while I can't say I'm going to grab a knife and stab the hunter, I don't want him to hurt shifters any more than you do. I can do this."

Jessup and Teddy looked at each other. Teddy shrugged, and Jessup decided he needed to have faith in his friend. If Hayes said he could do this, that meant he probably could.

"Let's go inside."

The first thing that hit Jessup when he opened the door was the smell. Frank had been sitting in here, tied to a chair, for several days. Whoever was on guard untied him a few times a day to allow him to go to the bathroom and to eat, but Frank hadn't had a shower for too long, and he'd had problems keeping his bowels under control the last time Jessup had been here. Frank didn't stand torture well, and the thought made Jessup smile wickedly.

Frank made a strangled sound and tried to push away from Jessup, but tied to the chair as he was, he wasn't going any-where. Jessup's smile widened, and he ignored the stench as he stepped in.

Hayes didn't do the same. He made a shocked face, then staggered back, one of his hands flying to his face. "What's that smell?" he asked.

"That's Frank."

"How can you stand to be in here?"

"I'm not going to be for long. Frank will tell me everything I want to know, right, Frank?" Jessup asked, turning to Frank.

"I'm not telling you sick fuck anything," Frank snarled, finding some of his courage.

It wouldn't last for long. Jessup came to a stop in front of Frank and used his ability. Frank couldn't move, and Jessup made sure he was aware of it. It was a finicky aspect of mind control, but he'd perfected it over the years. Frank stared at Hayes, maybe trying to get him to free him. He thought Hayes would have pity for him.

Unfortunately for Frank, he didn't know Hayes's back story. He didn't know that Hayes and his mate had adopted a little girl they'd freed from one of the labs. Hayes might have a soft heart, but he wanted revenge for his daughter and everyone else who'd been hurt.

"Do you know what they do in the labs?" Jessup asked.

"They get rid of you monsters," Frank answered.

"That's where you're wrong. We're not monsters when we're brought to those labs. We're monsters when we get out of them after they hurt us for weeks. That's what they do. They create monsters, but they don't kill them. They want super soldiers they can use against humans like you." Jessup reached for the knife he always carried with him. Frank's eyes widened, and he tried to get away again, but he didn't go anywhere.

He couldn't.

Jessup stepped closer and ran the tip of the knife up Frank's arm. "Are you in pain?" he asked casually.

"Don't hurt me again," Frank begged.

"Tell me what you know."

This time, Frank was eager to talk.

Rory was nervous, which didn't make sense. When had he ever been nervous around family?

But he hadn't seen his parents and siblings since he'd been kidnapped, and now, they were coming.

He wasn't an idiot. They'd said they wanted to make sure he was all right, but he knew there was a lot more behind it. His parents wanted to check in on him, meet Jessup, and ensure Rory wasn't making a mistake.

Rory was convinced he wasn't more than ever. He and Jessup were working things out slowly, but they weren't in a rush since he wasn't going anywhere. They could deal with their limitations and fears on their own time, which was all Rory wanted. He'd needed Jessup to give him a chance, and

Jessup was. Rory didn't want to mess that up and had no intention of moving back.

What would he be moving back to anyway? His family was there, but there was nothing else for him. He was sad to leave them behind, but he was an adult, and it wasn't like he'd been living at home with his parents. They'd still see each other, and it wouldn't even be hard. They could use one of those apps to have a Nix shimmer them around or even ask one of Rory's new friends.

In this case, Rikar had volunteered. Rory hadn't known what to make of it, considering who Rikar was, but something told him Rikar was the perfect man to send to his parents. He was calm and responsible and put people at ease. If he told Rory's parents he'd be there for Rory if he needed anything, it would put their minds at rest, which was what Rory wanted.

He didn't need his parents to accept that he was moving. He was doing it, whatever they thought of it. But after what they'd gone through with him being kidnapped and then not knowing what had happened to him, he didn't want them to be hurt more than they'd already been. He hoped they'd accept what he was doing, but he wasn't going back even if they didn't.

The past was the past, and being kidnapped had burned it all down. Now, Rory wanted to focus on his future, and that would happen in this town with Jessup by his side.

He twisted his fingers together as he waited by the front door. Rikar had said he'd shimmer Rory's family in front of the house where he and the other survivors lived, and Rory couldn't wait to see them. He bounced from foot to foot, having more energy than needed and no way to burn through it with his family about to arrive.

He told himself he didn't have a reason to be nervous, but any sensation of calmness he'd managed to dredge up flew out the window as soon as Rikar appeared in front of the house, Rory's family in tow.

They were here.

Rory beamed, unable to help himself. He launched himself down the stairs, almost falling on his face. Thankfully, his parents had been running toward him, and his father caught him and dragged him into his arms.

They wrapped around Rory in a way they never had, and he closed his eyes as he sank against his father's chest. He could feel his mother cling to him on his other side, and he wrapped an arm around her waist, holding her close.

His parents had been divorced for several years, but they hung onto each other and Rory as if they'd break into pieces if they didn't. Rory understood the sensation well because he felt the same way.

"I'm fine," he promised. "I'm safe, I swear."

"We thought we lost you," his mother said with a sob. She leaned back and rubbed her teary eyes. "Your father kept telling me you'd be fine, but I was so scared."

"You don't have to be anymore."

She looked him up and down. It wasn't easy since she was still hugging him, as was his father, but she managed.

Rory had made sure to pay extra attention to his appearance. He needed his family to believe that he was fine because he was. He had nightmares and no doubt that the kidnapping and knowing what would have been done to him would leave traces, but he'd deal with them when they arose. He wouldn't have to face them alone, either. Jessup would be there, as well as their friends.

Because Rory had friends here.

Something slammed against his back, and two arms wrapped around his waist from behind. He grabbed one of his sister's hands, squeezing it hard as she cried. He wanted to turn, but his father wouldn't let go. He had to wiggle until he managed to twist enough to get an arm around Carla's shoulders. That was when he noticed his brother and his cousin were there, too. He tilted his chin at them, and they ran forward.

The hug became a mess of arms and tears, but Rory wouldn't have it any other way. They all clung to each other, letting their fears go now that they could see Rory was truly all right. It took a little while, but eventually, the tears dried, and everyone relaxed.

Rory's mother looked around. "So where is that mate of yours?"

Jessup had mentioned talking to the hunter who'd kidnapped Rory, but Rory wasn't about to tell his mother that. He was pretty sure that talking wasn't what Jessup had in mind, and he didn't want to risk her asking for details.

"He's working, but he'll come around eventually."

She nodded, but she still looked worried. "Are you sure about this? I realize he's your mate and that you want to be with him, but you've been through a lot. Maybe your feelings are running a bit too high for you to make such drastic decisions."

She wasn't telling Rory to come home. She was just worried about him, and he understood why. He was grateful for how much his mother cared about him. Jessup didn't have that, and it wasn't fair.

"Tell me about him, then," she ordered as she hooked an arm around Rory's elbow.

Rikar had vanished, no doubt to give them time together. Rory wasn't sure where he'd gone, but he gestured at his family to come into the house.

"This is where they take all the survivors. I've been staying here, but now that I've decided to move here permanently, I'll be able to find a home for myself," he explained.

"Will you be moving in with your mate?" his father asked.

The entire family was stuck close, and Rory decided to take them to the living room. There would be enough space for everyone to sit. "We haven't talked about that yet, so I don't think so. Jessup shares a house with friends, too, though. If he decides he wants to move in with me at a later date, it won't be a problem."

"He doesn't want to live with you?" Carla asked.

"That's not what I said, but Jessup has a hard time opening up." Rory hesitated. He didn't want to tell Jessup's secrets, but he needed his family to understand. "He wasn't as lucky as I was. When he was kidnapped, his family didn't care. They didn't look for him, and he only went back once after he was released."

"He was kidnapped, too?" Rory's mother asked.

"Just like I was. I was lucky because he and his friends stopped the people who took me before they could hurt me, but Jessup was experimented on." Rory's family knew about the labs. It was an important part of the history of the supernatural world, and his parents had made sure Rory and his siblings knew what was happening, even though they'd been young when the scandal had come to light.

Everyone looked horrified. Rory wasn't sure if it was because of what had happened to Jessup or what could have happened to him, but it didn't matter.

"He had to get through it on his own?" Rory's mother asked. She still clung to him, so when he sat on the couch, she sat next to him and linked their fingers together.

"Not alone. He became close to other people who were in the labs. They stuck together because all of them came out with new abilities. They use those abilities to free more people."

"What ability does your mate have?" Rory's brother asked.

Rory and Jessup had agreed that Rory could tell his family what Jessup could do. Some people had a problem with it, and Jessup wanted them to know before they met. Rory wanted to believe his family wouldn't care, but he knew his mother, so he knew where her mind would go.

Still, he sucked in a breath. "He can control people with his mind. It's like in the movies, I guess."

There was a moment of silence, and Rory waited. Just like he'd expected, his mother was the first to speak. "What if he used that ability on you?" she asked.

Rory sighed. He'd known his mother would be afraid of that. It wouldn't be easy to convince her that wasn't the case, but he was ready to do just that—or at least try.

"Nothing new, then?" Moore asked.

Jessup shook his head. "He gave us a few new names, but I doubt they're anyone important. He wasn't recruited long ago and hasn't been doing much except kidnapping shifters and delivering them to the labs."

"Give me those names anyway," Moore ordered.

He was behind his desk, which was an odd sight. Moore didn't used to have an office, but then, they didn't use to have a home. Before, they'd lived in abandoned warehouses and whatever places with enough space for all of them. That had changed after Moore had met his mate. Jolyn worked with the council assassins, and through them, the mutants found a home with Rikar and his tribe. Moore was still annoyed at that, but even though he acted as if he barely tolerated the assassins, Jessup knew better. Those people had saved their lives, whether or not they were willing to accept it. Jessup had no doubt that someone in their group would have eventually gotten hurt. They wouldn't have had anyone to ask for help, and they might have lost someone.

But now, the mutants had a home. Moore shared a house with his mate, while Hayes had moved in with Rikar. It made

Jessup wonder if maybe he and Rory should move in to-gether, too. He kind of wanted to, but it was too soon. Their relationship was still shaky, and he wasn't quite sure how to live with his mate. He didn't have any problem living with the other mutants, but that was different.

He wasn't falling in love with any of them.

Moore pinched the bridge of his nose and leaned back in his chair. "I don't think we're equipped to deal with the hunt-ers."

Jessup was surprised to hear him admit that. He and Hayes exchanged a glance, but they both stayed silent.

Moore straightened. "I'm going to have to call in the assas-sins."

"I didn't think I'd ever hear you say that," Hayes teased.

Moore glared at him without heat. "We can't focus on eve-rything at once. Besides, the raids on the labs will become more dangerous for us and the people we rescue if these hunt-ers are involved. We were lucky that there were only three of them this time, but two got away. We have to assume they went straight to their leader, whoever that is, and told them about us. That means they most likely know someone is raid-ing the labs if they didn't already."

Jessup was glad he wasn't the one in charge because he wouldn't have known what to do. Thankfully, their relation-ship with the assassins had become more relaxed since Moore and Jolyn had bonded, and hopefully, the assassins would be willing to help.

"Thank you for letting me know about this," Moore said, already reaching for his phone. "I'll let you know what the assassins say."

That was a dismissal if Jessup had ever heard one, and he was eager to go. He had things to do and places to be, even though it all terrified him.

Rory's family was in town.

He'd known it would happen eventually. They wanted to see Rory, and since he'd decided he was moving here, their visit had been a given. They wanted to reassure themselves that he was all right, and when they'd found out he wasn't going to them, they'd decided to come to him.

But them being in town meant Jessup would have to meet them. He'd wondered if he could avoid it but realized he couldn't. What would it say about him if he didn't want to meet his mate's parents? Jessup didn't need them to like him, but he still wanted to make a good impression. If things went the way they should, these people would be part of his life for decades. He couldn't afford to antagonize them, especially when things were still shaky with Rory, and it was entirely Jessup's fault.

Jessup was still hesitant as he and Hayes left Moore's house. He didn't have a way out of meeting Rory's parents, but that didn't mean he was looking forward to doing so. If anything, he was terrified. What if they didn't like him? What if they told Rory he needed to let him go? It would probably be for the best, at least for Rory, but Jessup wasn't sure he could survive that. He'd finally opened up to Rory, and it had only taken a handful of dates for Rory to worm his way into Jessup's heart. Now, he was firmly wedged there, and Jessup wasn't sure what he'd do if Rory decided to go home.

"Do you want to come over for lunch?" Hayes asked.

"I don't think I can."

Hayes frowned. "Why not?" He seemed to realize something and grinned. "You have something planned with your mate?"

It was still strange to hear that word linked to Jessup. "Not exactly. Rory's family is in town visiting him."

"So you're already at the meeting the family step?"

"It's not like he'll meet mine, but I guess we are."

Hayes grimaced. "From the little you've said, it's a good

thing he's not going to meet your family."

That would have been a disaster, mostly because they wouldn't have cared who Rory was. They wouldn't have wanted to make a good impression.

For the first time, Jessup was actually glad they weren't in his life anymore. He didn't know if they'd have ruined everything, but it would have been a risk, but it wasn't a risk he needed to take.

"What if they don't like me?" he asked Hayes. After all, his friend had met Rikar's family. He'd probably been just as scared as Jessup was.

"Then, they don't like you. They're not the ones who have to be bonded to you."

"But they won't want Rory to be with me if they don't like me."

"And if he's the guy I believe he is, he won't care."

"He loves them. I don't want him to lose them because of me."

"I hope he won't, but even if he does lose them, it won't be your fault. It'll be theirs, and you have to accept that. You can't carry the weight of this on your shoulders when you don't have to, Jessup. I know Leon told you this before, but Rory needs to make his own decisions. If he chooses you over his family, then feel humbled by that and love him for it. That's all you can do."

Hayes was right, but it didn't mean Jessup still wasn't terrified. He wouldn't get out of this, though, so after saying goodbye, he headed toward the house where Rory still lived with the other survivors. Most of them had gone home or moved to their own place, including Alma, the woman who'd been in the van with Rory, and Jessup wondered if Rory would want to leave eventually. He'd said he was moving to town, so he wouldn't be going far, but what would Jessup do then? Would he move in with Rory? Would Rory even want him to?

That was one more thing they needed to talk about, dammit.

Jessup reached the house and walked in, but froze before stepping into the living room. He could hear Rory and his family talking, and of course, the topic of the conversation was him.

"You can't know that for sure," a woman said.

"I can. He's my mate, and he would never hurt me that way."

"But don't you see? You wouldn't even realize it if he did."

Jessup swallowed. Clearly, Rory had told his family about Jessup's ability. It didn't seem to have gone well, and Jessup took a step back, ready to leave. It was better to give Rory time and space to talk to his family.

As he turned, a woman he didn't know appeared from the hallway, drying her hands on her jeans. Her long brown hair framed her round face, and after drying her hands, she pushed her glasses up her nose. Her eyes widened when she saw him, and he wondered what she'd think if he ran out the door.

"You're Jessup," she whispered.

Jessup wasn't sure why she was speaking so softly, but he nodded and kept silent.

The woman beamed. "I just wanted to tell you that I'm on your side. I don't care what my mother thinks. You shouldn't care about it, either. She worries about Rory, but he'll show her this is right for him. Besides, you're his mate. You were meant for him, which means this is right."

Jessup had no idea who the woman was, but he was glad that at least one person in Rory's family was on his side.

When Carla came back from the bathroom, she wasn't alone.

Jessup looked like he'd rather be anywhere but here and was seriously contemplating jumping out the window, which Rory took as a sign that he'd heard what his mother had been saying.

Shit.

He shot up from the couch, eager to make sure Jessup knew he didn't think he was controlling him with his mind or in any other way. "Jessup. You're here."

Jessup hovered by the living room door. "Yeah. I, uh, I told you I'd meet your family."

Rory's mother looked horrified. Rory normally would have hated that, but she wouldn't listen to him. She was desperate to get him to come home, and she knew he wouldn't as long as Jessup was in his life. She wasn't trying to separate them, just to get Rory to doubt that he and Jessup could be together right after the trauma he'd been through. She wanted to protect him and enfold him back into the family, and while he understood, she needed to see that he'd already made his decision. He'd chosen what his future would be like, and who it would be with.

Jessup.

Jessup didn't bolt when Rory reached him. He allowed Rory to take his hand and pull him toward his family, who all got to their feet. Rory's cousin was the first to offer Jessup his hand. He beamed at Rory's mate, letting Jessup and Rory know he was on their side.

"I'm Marcus, and I don't know how to thank you for saving Rory."

Jessup rubbed the back of his neck. "Anyone would have done the same thing."

"Maybe so, but I think it's fitting that the two of you are mates. Rory told us you were the one who got him out of that van."

"We work as a team. I might have been the one there, but we all worked together to get the prisoners out of the lab and make sure the scientists can't hurt anyone else."

Rory didn't want them to go down that path because his mother would be horrified. She wouldn't understand that the scientists needed to be killed, but Rory did. He wasn't willing to let her push Jessup away, no matter why she did it.

He cleared his throat and gestured at his parents. "This is my father, Rupert, and my mother, Eliza. You already met my sister, apparently, so the only one left is my brother Quentin."

Carla and Marcus were firmly on Rory and Jessup's side. Rory's father was a bit more hesitant, while Quentin and Rory's mother wanted Rory to come home and leave Jessup behind. Quentin had suggested that Rory could come back later, once he'd recovered, but he didn't understand that Rory wouldn't recover if he left. Jessup had become his rock, and he needed his mate and his family to get along. He didn't want to have to choose between the two.

"It's a pleasure to meet all of you," Jessup said.

He seemed less freaked out now, which was good. Rory clung to him, needing to reassure him that whatever happened, he'd already chosen him. No matter how much it would hurt, he wouldn't go along with what his mother and brother wanted because it was wrong for him.

Rory wouldn't force Jessup to stay here for long. He'd wanted his mate and his family to meet, but even though he and Jessup weren't bonded, he could feel the anxiousness radiating from his mate's body.

Thankfully, he wasn't the only one, and his father took pity on both Rory and Jessup. "Why don't we head to the bed and breakfast?" he suggested, looking around the room. "I don't know about you, but I'd like the opportunity to freshen up. We can meet Rory and Jessup tomorrow."

Rory's mother looked like she was about to protest, but Carla stepped in. "And I'm dying to explore the town. It's really cute, and I can see why Rory wants to move here."

"I know what the two of you are doing," Rory's mother grumbled. "But fine. Let's go. Rory, we'll see you tomorrow?"

Rory nodded. "Of course." His family wouldn't stay for more than a few days, but clearly, everyone needed time to wrap their minds around meeting Jessup and what his presence in Rory's life meant. Rory hoped his mother would be more understanding after she had time to think about who Jessup was and what he meant to Rory.

Rory and Jessup walked Rory's family to the front door. They watched them leave, and Rory could feel Jessup relax next to him the further away his family was. He almost laughed because he knew they were a lot, but they weren't going anywhere, and hopefully, Jessup would get used to their presence. It wasn't like they lived close by, so maybe the distance would help Jessup learn to accept them.

"I'm sorry," Jessup said as soon as Rory's family was far enough that they wouldn't hear him.

Rory faced him. "You have nothing to be sorry about. You heard what my mother said?"

Jessup nodded. He was doing his best not to look at Rory, so Rory cupped one of his cheeks. He didn't force him to look, but the skin-to-skin contact helped him feel more grounded. "I don't agree with her. I don't believe you're using your ability to control me. I don't think you've ever used it outside one of the labs or in similar situations. You wouldn't do that, especially not to me."

"I swear I wouldn't."

Jessup finally looked at Rory, and Rory kissed him. He needed Jessup to believe him, but he also needed more for himself. Having his mother push for him to leave his mate behind hadn't felt good, and Rory could tell Jessup thought that, eventually, he'd say yes. Why wouldn't he? Going home would mean he was back with his family, and Jessup craved that kind of connection.

But Rory craved something else.

"I want us to bond," he whispered.

The shock made Jessup's entire body tense. "What?"

He didn't push Rory away, so Rory gathered his courage and continued. "I want us to bond. I don't see a reason to wait, and I think you'll be more comfortable once you're able to feel what I feel. You'll also know that I won't leave you if we're bonded."

"I don't want you to do this just because you're trying to reassure me."

"But don't you see? I'm also trying to reassure myself. All of this feels unreal. A week ago, I was living my life, and everything has changed. I can't ever go back, and I don't want to. I want to move forward, and I'll only do that with you. We're mates, and to me, the bond means everything. I don't want to rush you if you're truly not ready for this, but if you're saying no because you think I'll regret it, please stop. I made my decision. I chose you, not my past. I want you, and nothing will change my mind."

Jessup stared at Rory while Rory prayed he'd say yes. He'd known he risked sending Jessup running with this offer, but he wanted Jessup to accept that they were an item and that he wouldn't abandon him the way his family did. He wasn't going anywhere.

"All right."

Rory blinked. He'd expected Jessup to say no and to continue trying to protect him from himself, but he wasn't about to protest. Yes was the answer he'd wanted to hear.

He beamed and pulled Jessup toward the stairs. He felt Jessup stumble, but he was eager to get him upstairs. "The house is empty," he explained as they climbed the stairs.

"Did you have this planned?"

"Not really. I knew I wanted to bond with you, but the house being empty is because most of the survivors went home."

"You didn't."

Rory reached the top of the stairs and turned to face Jessup. "That's because I'm already home. Home is wherever you are."

That seemed to make something snap in Jessup. He swallowed, then swooped forward and grabbed Rory by the waist. He was strong. Rory had no trouble wrapping his legs around Jessup's waist. They kissed as Jessup pressed Rory's back against the wall, but it wasn't enough. The bond wasn't complete, and there was nothing Rory wanted more.

He gestured toward his bedroom, hoping Jessup would get the message.

He did.

Jessup pushed them away from the wall and staggered in the direction Rory had indicated. He never let go of Rory, and Rory clung to him, making it obvious it was perfectly fine with him.

They finally reached his bedroom. He struggled to open the door, but once he managed, he pushed it all the way, tightening his legs around Jessup to let him know he needed to move. Jessup did, kicking the door closed behind himself and making a beeline for the bed. He hesitated for a moment once he reached it, maybe because he didn't want to dump Rory like a sack of potatoes, but Rory didn't care. He wiggled until Jessup let him go, and as soon as he landed on the mattress, he tugged off his sweater.

Jessup laughed. It wasn't a sound Rory had heard often, and it startled him enough that he stopped moving to look up at his mate. Jessup sheepishly shrugged, still smiling.

"I like that you're that eager to be with me."

Rory settled on his knees and kissed his mate. "You haven't seen eager yet. Get naked."

Rory didn't check to see if Jessup obeyed. He focused on

taking off his clothes, wanting to be naked as soon as possible. Jessup wasn't as fast, and by the time Rory was naked, he was still working on his jeans.

Rory glared at him. "You're killing me. Come on, Jessup." He reached for Jessup's chest, tweaking a nipple.

"*Rory,*" Jessup gasped as his back arched. That was the reaction Rory wanted, but it didn't get Jessup any more naked.

"I want us to bond, Jessup. We can do it without sex, but it's not what I had in mind."

Jessup nodded eagerly and finally managed to push his jeans down his legs. Rory wrapped his hand around his mate's dick as soon as it was free. He'd dreamed of this moment, and now, he was living it.

Jessup's hips jerked forward, and he paused again, letting Rory do what he wanted, which was slowly jacking off his mate. It wasn't nearly enough, but it was so damn good to be able to touch him.

Rory rose on his knees to nose along Jessup's collarbone. He paused there to suck a mark, in anticipation of the bite he'd put there later. He rumbled with satisfaction at the redness and the moan coming from Jessup.

Rory took Jessup's hand and pulled. Jessup came, his eyes wide, his cheeks flushed, more gorgeous than Rory had ever seen him and all Rory's.

They stretched out on the mattress, but before settling down into Jessup's arms—or under him—Rory rolled toward his nightstand. He'd gone shopping recently because he'd wanted to be ready for this when it happened.

"You really want this, don't you?" Jessup asked when Rory rolled back toward him.

Rory couldn't hold back anymore. He'd never felt so possessive and like he *needed* someone. He didn't even care that it was because of the bond. He just cared that he and Jessup were forever. "You're mine, Jessup. That's never going to change, and I'll work as hard as I can to show you that I'll never leave you."

Because that was what Jessup was afraid of. His family had abandoned him, and he expected Rory to do the same.

Never.

"Only yours," Jessup agreed.

He took the lube from Rory's hand but waited for Rory to nod to open it. Rory knew what he wanted and what he enjoyed, and he couldn't wait for Jessup to fuck and bite him. Thankfully, he didn't have to wait long. Now that they were doing this, Jessup seemed as impatient as Rory.

He opened the lube and quickly slicked his fingers. Rory thought about the best way to do this, but really, he just wanted Jessup inside him. He decided to roll over, then scooted back against Jessup's chest. Jessup got what Rory was trying to do and helped him hook his thigh over his, opening his body up. He ran slick fingers along Rory's hip, then between his legs. He ignored Rory's cock, which made Rory whine, then moan when Jessup's fingers found his hole.

This. This was what he wanted. It was what he *needed.*

Rory whined and pushed against Jessup's fingers. Jessup seemed to have infinite patience as he got Rory ready and ignored all attempts Rory made to rush him. He stretched Rory's body to welcome him, and at the same time, he kissed and sucked on Rory's neck, right where he was about to bite.

This really was the perfect position.

Rory couldn't take it anymore. He needed more, which meant Jessup had to move *now.* Rory wasn't sure how to make his mate realize that, so he rolled his head and caught Jessup's left bicep with his teeth. He didn't bite hard, but the threat was obvious, and it made Jessup laugh. The rumbling of his chest made Rory shake, and he let go to turn his head and glare.

"Now," he ordered.

Jessup seemed amused. He didn't let Rory rush him,

instead making sure Rory truly was ready for him. When Rory tried to look at him again, he bit down on Rory's neck, causing him to freeze.

They both were on edge. Rory could feel Jessup's hard cock pressing between his ass cheeks, and he wiggled his hips, trying to get it to slip inside of him. "What are you waiting for?" he whined.

Jessup finally gave Rory what he wanted. Rory felt him tilt his head back, and he pushed back against him, the head of his cock caught against Rory's hole. Rory's eyes fluttered closed, and he pushed back, groaning at the sensation of Jessup sliding inside of him.

"Want you," he whispered.

"You have me."

"Forever?" Maybe Rory was a little bit insecure, too.

Jessup didn't answer with words. He pressed his face against Rory's neck, and Rory felt his fangs sink into his flesh. He tensed, but Jessup was great at distracting him with his cock. He fucked into Rory as he drank down Rory's blood, and Rory clutched at Jessup's arm. He'd wrapped both of them around Rory and was holding Rory still against him as he fucked him, which was really freaking hot, but Rory had finally realized the disadvantage of this position.

He couldn't bite Jessup.

Well, he couldn't bite Jessup's neck, but there was one part of him he could reach.

Rory's fangs tingled as they came down. He tightened his hold on Jessup's arm and brought it to his mouth, biting down on the meaty part of Jessup's bicep. Jessup jerked against Rory's back, his cock pushing deeper into Rory, but Rory focused on the blood filling his mouth.

It was warm and coppery and the one thing that would link him and Jessup for the rest of their lives.

Jessup whimpered a little and withdrew his fangs. Rory

continued drinking. He could feel the bond between them become tighter, pulling them together until they were one, and pleasure exploded. It coursed through the bond, creating a feedback loop between the two of them. Jessup cried out and his rhythm stuttered, then he pushed hard into Rory. Rory could feel him coming, and it triggered his own orgasm.

He let go of Jessup's arm and threw his head back, almost hitting Jessup's nose. Jessup didn't complain, probably because he was too busy coming again in answer to Rory's orgasm.

Jessup groaned and tightened his hold on Rory as if he never wanted to let go. The pleasure felt like too much, but eventually, it slowed down.

Rory could feel deep happiness coming through the bond, and he felt the same way. It was them against the world now, forever.

He slumped against the pillow as Jessup raised his hand. The outline of Rory's teeth was stark on Jessup's skin, and the sight made Rory smile.

"On the arm, Rory?" Jessup asked.

"In hindsight, this wasn't the best position."

Jessup pushed his hips forward. His cock was softening, but he was still inside Rory, and the sensation was delicious. "I kind of like it."

Rory moaned. "Me, too."

Perfect position, after all.

CHAPTER SIX

The bond had settled something in Jessup. He hadn't expected it, but he probably should have. Knowing what Rory felt made reading his moods and fears easier, which meant that Jessup knew how to react. He couldn't tell *why* Rory felt the way he did, but a quick conversation with his mate usually was enough to smooth out his fears and make him feel better.

It would take some time to get used to all of this, but Jessup was convinced that bonding so quickly would benefit both of them. He had no doubt Rory's mother would have something to say about that, but thankfully, she'd kept her thoughts to herself when she'd seen them the day after they'd bonded. She'd known it was too late and that Rory had made his decision. There would be no going back, but she probably hadn't expected either of them to want to. Even though she wasn't convinced Jessup wouldn't hurt Rory, he was Rory's mate, and in the end, that was all that mattered.

A knock on the door made Jessup frown. He wasn't expecting anyone, and the other mutants usually didn't bother to knock. They still came in without hesitation even though they didn't live here. Someone was there, though, and Jessup quickly dried his hands on a kitchen towel and went to open it. He expected someone he knew on the other side of the door, and he'd been right. He just hadn't thought it would be two council assassins.

He blinked at them. "Somehow, I don't think I'm the person you were looking for."

One of the assassins, a Nix, grinned. "Not unless you're Moore, and I already know you're not because we met before. I'm Dasha."

Jessup vaguely remembered him from one of the meetings they'd had with the assassins. Back then, though, he'd been more focused on the thought that the assassins could probably kill them with barely a thought.

Jessup offered Dasha his hand. "I remember. I'm Jessup. Let me call Moore to let him know you're here." He cocked his head. "Can I ask why you're here?"

"To pick up your prisoner. Moore already knows about it, but we weren't sure where to find him. We thought this was the place."

"No, that would be the house two houses down from this one."

"At least we didn't get it too wrong." He gestured at the man standing next to him. "This is Ulric."

Jessup nodded at him as he took out his phone to call Moore. Luckily, Moore had been expecting the assassins. "Can you take them to Frank?" he asked. "I have to finish something before meeting with them."

"Not a problem."

"Thank you. I'll be glad to be rid of Frank."

"I'm pretty sure we all feel that way." Mostly because Frank didn't have any useful information, and Jessup was done dealing with him. He was still pissed because Frank had kidnapped Rory, but he'd promised Moore he wouldn't kill the guy. He hadn't been sure why Moore didn't want him to, but it made more sense now that he knew the assassins were involved.

They were about to leave when the bond told Jessup Rory was close. He looked around, grinning, when he noticed his mate hovering close by, clearly unsure whether or not he should join them.

Rory smiled back and quickly climbed the porch steps, coming straight for Jessup. Jessup didn't hesitate to wrap an arm around his shoulders and pull him close to kiss the top of his head, even though they were in front of two relative strangers.

"This is my mate, Rory," Jessup told them. "Rory, these are two of the council assassins, Dasha and Ulric."

Rory knew about the council assassins because Jessup had explained who they were and what they did. Rory was a bit hesitant, but he'd explained he understood the need for them. Living with the survivors, he'd heard enough horror stories of what happened in the labs.

Rory nodded at them. "Pleasure to meet you."

Dasha smiled at him. "It's good to see another one of the mutants have found his mate."

Rory frowned. "You know, I don't like that word much."

"Neither do I, but it's what they call themselves."

Rory had mentioned to Jessup that he didn't like that word, and it made sense because he wasn't one of them. He didn't know what it felt like to have been changed that way, and Jessup didn't have anything against the word. He was a mutant. He wasn't just a shifter anymore, and he certainly wasn't fully human. He was something other, and mutant fit that as well as any other word might. At least this way, people understood right away that he was different.

Jessup didn't view his ability as something bad. The way it had been forced on him certainly was, as would have been the way the humans would have wanted him to use it, but he was his own person. He wasn't a prisoner anymore, and no one would ever force him to do anything he didn't want.

He'd just control their mind if they tried.

"They're here to pick up Frank," Jessup explained because he knew Rory would want to know.

Rory nodded. "It's about time."

They'd talked about this, so Jessup knew he didn't like having Frank so close, even though the guy hadn't hurt him. None of them wanted the hunter to stick around. The town was their home, and they needed to be able to feel safe here.

"I agree," Jessup said. "I'll walk them there. I'll be right back, all right?"

"I'll come with you."

Jessup stared, sure he'd misunderstood. Why would Rory want to see Frank?

Maybe he had questions for him. After all, even though Frank hadn't hurt him, he'd kidnapped him, and he wouldn't have hesitated to hand Rory over to the scientists in the lab. If Rory needed to see Frank to get some closure, then Jessup was fine with him coming along. He didn't like it, but he also wouldn't try to change Rory's mind. He deserved to heal, even if Jessup disagreed with how he did it.

"Let's go," he said, gesturing toward the other side of town.

The place where they kept Frank was as far away from the survivors as possible, but it took them only a few minutes to get there. The town wasn't that big yet, even though it was steadily growing.

Their small group was silent as they walked, but as soon as the small wooden structure appeared, that changed. Leon was guarding Frank today, but he wasn't standing by the door. Instead, he was flat on his face with a pool of blood around his head.

Before Jessup could say anything, Rory started running. Jessup called him back, but Rory ignored him, and Jessup knew why. Leon was one of the people who'd saved him and a friend, and if there was anything he could do to help him, he'd do it, even if it put him in danger.

"I'm calling Moore," Jessup said. They needed to get their people here ASAP.

Rory had knelt next to Leon, but he seemed afraid to touch him. "Leon?" he asked gently.

As soon as Jessup was done explaining what happened to Moore, he put his phone away and looked into the structure. He wasn't surprised to see the chair was empty and that there was no sign of Frank. "We need to find him," he said.

Ulric nodded. "I'll shift into my wolf form. He has to be in the forest somewhere."

"I'll look for him from the sky." This was the one time Jessup's ability to turn into an owl would come in handy.

They needed to find Frank before he did something stupid like attacking someone.

"I'll shimmer him to the infirmary," Dasha said as he crouched next to Rory and Leon.

Rory nodded. Leon was unconscious, and there was no way to tell what had happened to him. Well, beyond the blow to the back of his head. That seemed to be where most of the blood came from, but Rory wasn't sure. He was too afraid to touch Leon in case he did more bad than good.

When Dasha grabbed Leon's shoulder, Rory pushed away. He didn't want to be in the way, and Leon needed more medical attention than he could help with. Hell, he felt queasy at the sight of so much blood, and when Dasha shimmered Leon away, Rory couldn't help but stare at the pool of sticky red on the ground. His mouth filled with saliva, and he forced himself to his feet.

He looked around. He was alone now, with both Ulric and Jessup having left to try to find the hunter. Rory didn't like being here on his own, and the thought of what might happen made him shiver. He had no doubt that hunter was as far away as possible from here as he could be by now, but still. He felt like he was being watched, and it was creeping him out.

Rory rubbed his hands on his thighs. He'd wait for Jessup at home.

He never made it there. He took a step toward the path that would lead him back into town proper when a rustling in the bushes made him tense. He stared, knowing what was about to happen.

The hunter stumbled from between the trees. There was blood running down his cheek, and his eyes were wide, but he was steady on his feet, which meant that when he saw Rory, he made a beeline for him. Rory looked around, desperately trying to find a place to hide, or at the very least, a place where he could stay until Jessup came back, but there was nowhere but the small structure behind him, and he wasn't setting foot in there.

Frank grabbed Rory's arm and pulled him closer. The stench was enough to make Rory's eyes burn. He gagged, wondering what Frank would do if he threw up on him.

"They left you here?" Frank asked.

Rory glared at him and pulled on his arm, but Frank wasn't an idiot. He didn't let go. "They're going to kill you when they find out you put your hands on me."

Frank grinned. There was blood on his teeth, too. Even though Leon had gone down, it seemed he'd tried to defend himself first. He'd gotten in a few good hits by the sight of it, and it gave Rory immense satisfaction.

Frank gave him a shake, making Rory's teeth rattle. "Shut up. You're my ticket out of here."

Rory snorted. "Yeah? And how do you think you're going to leave?"

"If anyone finds us, I'll use you as a hostage. Now shut up. I need to find out where to go."

Frank looked around. Rory could almost see what was going on in his mind. He needed to get away from town, but he didn't know where anything was. He'd been blindfolded when he'd been brought here, which meant he had no idea where he was. Rory supposed that was where he came in, but he wasn't about to tell Frank anything. He doubted Frank would hurt him, and if he tried, Rory would just shift and run.

He was tempted to do it right away, but he was also afraid. What if Frank found someone else to use as a hostage? There were kids in town, and Rory couldn't put them in danger. It was better if Frank used him.

Even though it was very far from the idea Rory had of fun.

Frank gave Rory another shake and pulled him toward the path. "I need a car," he muttered.

"You need more than a car. You're going to need an ambulance when my mate realizes what you've done."

Frank stumbled. "Your mate?"

"Yep. Remember the guy who knocked you on your ass back at the lab? That's him."

Rory couldn't be sure because of how dirty and bloody Frank was, but he was pretty sure the human had just paled. "The asshole who tortured me?" Frank asked.

"Him," Rory confirmed.

He'd known Jessup had tortured Frank. He didn't like the idea of it, but he also understood that Jessup and the others had been trying to get answers. There were still so many labs out there, with scientists hurting shifters and humans alike. If they had to torture an asshole to get answers out of him and save lives, then Rory was all for it.

Especially if that asshole had kidnapped him not once but twice now.

Frank appeared to make a decision. Instead of taking the path like he'd started earlier, he dragged Rory toward the forest, which wasn't the smartest idea. There were at least two shifters in there trying to find Frank.

Rory kept his mouth shut. Frank clearly wasn't the

brightest crayon in the box. Hopefully, this meant Jessup would find Rory soon. Rory was doing his best not to allow the panic he felt to leak through the bond, but he wasn't sure he was doing a good job. He didn't want Jessup to freak out, but he also wouldn't allow Frank to take him away from town. It would be the worst thing that could happen, and Frank had already hurt Rory once. Rory wouldn't let the asshole hurt him a second time.

Besides, Rory had a plan. He didn't care what Frank thought of his shifted form, and he wouldn't hesitate to use it now that they were headed away from town.

He waited until they were in the forest. Frank kept looking around, entirely lost. He was distracted enough that Rory knew this was his chance. He allowed the shift to wash over him, reaching out to his antelope, welcoming it and the protection it could give him. He'd be smaller in his antelope form, and hopefully, that meant he'd manage to get away from Frank.

Frank yelped when Rory's arm shrunk in his hold. He snatched his hand away and stumbled back, and Rory finished shifting. It was uncomfortable to shift while he was dressed, but he managed to shake off his jeans. His t-shirt was stuck, but it shouldn't be a problem, or at least, he hoped it wouldn't be.

"What the fuck are you doing?" Frank demanded to know.

Rory stared at him. Surely, Frank didn't expect him to answer. He had to realize that Rory couldn't in this form.

"And what the fuck are you?" Frank asked, taking a step back.

Rory glared at him, but he wasn't going to stick around and explain what he was. Frank was the last person whose opinion he cared about, especially when it came to his shifted form. After one last glance, Rory turned and started running, abandoning his clothes and everything else behind. He heard

Frank cry out, but he didn't stop to check what had happened to the human.

He could die for all Rory cared about.

Rory ran. He had no idea where he was going, but he could hear Frank coming after him. He doubted the human could catch up to him, but his heart still raced as he wound around trees and bushes. In this form, he could hide somewhere, but he needed a few moments so Frank couldn't see where, and that might be a problem.

Frank cried out, and Rory turned to see a bundle of brown feathers dive-bomb Frank's face. Frank screamed, stumbled back, and fell on his ass as the owl attacked again.

Rory was safe. Jessup was here, and he'd take care of him.

And of Frank.

Rory huddled against a tree, staring at the owl coming down time and time again, scratching Frank's face, his hands, and any patch of skin he could get to. Frank was screaming as if he were burning alive, which Rory thought was a bit dramatic, but at least it meant the others would easily find them.

It would be a good thing for Frank, too, because unless Rory was wrong, Jessup had every intention of scratching Frank to death. He didn't understand why Jessup wasn't using his ability, but it wasn't like he could ask in this form, and he wasn't planning on shifting back anytime soon. He needed to be able to run quickly if he had to, although he doubted Frank would be a problem for much longer.

Jessup would make sure he wasn't.

Jessup was pissed. Attacking the human with his claws was much more satisfying than using his ability, which was why he wasn't using mind control on Frank. He would, eventually, but he wasn't done drawing blood yet. Jessup didn't know how Rory would react after seeing him like this, but he couldn't stop. He needed to make Frank pay for what he'd done.

He'd taken Jessup's mate.

Jessup couldn't remember ever being so angry. How dare Frank put his hands on Rory? How dare he threaten one of the few people who cared about Jessup? Jessup wouldn't allow him to do anything to Rory, and he'd make sure Frank regretted what he'd already done.

Jessup was going to tear him apart.

Or at least, that was the plan until Teddy shimmered next to them, Moore by his side. Jessup barely looked at him. Instead, he divebombed Frank's face again, screeching as he did so. Frank was trying to cover his face with his arms, which were full of long bloody scratches. It was really fucking satisfying, but Jessup wasn't done yet.

"Stop," Moore ordered.

Jessup did. Even though technically, he and the other mutants were part of Rikar's tribe now, Moore had always been his alpha, albeit unofficially. Moore would hate to have anyone call him that, but he'd been guiding and protecting them since they'd left the labs. Even though he didn't like the word, he *was* their alpha, and Jessup found himself compelled to obey his order.

He landed, glaring from Moore to Frank. He took a step forward, wondering if maybe he could get one last scratch in, but Moore pointed his finger at him. "Stay there. He's not going anywhere, and he'll need his tongue still attached to answer the assassins' questions."

"The assassins?" Frank asked, his voice trembling.

Jessup would have grinned if he'd been in his human form. He hadn't gotten much out of Frank, but now, the professionals were stepping in. Frank would regret not giving Jessup what he'd wanted.

Jessup shifted. Frank made a strangled sound and tried to

push himself to his feet, but Teddy kicked him in the ribs. Everyone was pissed, and things would only get worse for Frank.

"Where's Leon?" Jessup asked. "He was wounded. Is he okay?"

"Dasha shimmered him away," Rory said from behind Jessup.

Jessup turned toward him. Both of them were naked, but they didn't care. They stared at each other for a moment before Jessup opened his arms. Rory cried out and launched himself at him, and Jessup wrapped himself around his mate.

He should have kept Rory safe, but he'd failed. Hopefully, Rory would forgive him.

Ulric arrived after only a few seconds, still in his wolf form, quickly followed by Dasha, who shimmered in with a tall man Jessup vaguely remembered. Moore was on them in seconds, asking about Leon, but a movement at the corner of his eye caught Jessup's attention.

Frank was trying to run, the asshole.

Ulric placed himself in front of Frank, snarling and showing Frank his teeth. Frank looked like he might decide to face Ulric as long as it took him as far away from the assassins as possible, but Jessup wouldn't allow him to go anywhere.

Using his ability, he froze Frank in place. He'd done it enough times that it was easy for him to ensure that Frank understood what was going on around him. When he used his ability on children or on the survivors of the labs, he didn't want them to remember, so he made sure they didn't. He couldn't take away the memories of what had been done to them, but he could make sure they couldn't remember being mind-controlled.

With Frank, he didn't care. He *wanted* Frank to remember all of this.

Jessup let go of Rory, even though there was nothing he

wanted less, and stepped closer to Frank. Frank didn't move because he couldn't, and Jessup grinned at him.

"You feel that?" he asked softly, leaning closer. "I'm controlling your body, and I could make you do anything I want." To show Frank that he wasn't kidding, he forced him to raise a hand. He made Frank tap his temple with one finger, and he knew Frank understood what he was threatening because he shuddered.

"I could make you kill yourself," Jessup continued. "That would be nice to watch after what you've done to my mate and one of my best friends. How do you think I should do it? A gun would be too fast, wouldn't it? It wouldn't let you experience enough pain, so that would be out. Maybe a knife? I could make you stab yourself time and time again, starting from your thighs, then moving up your body. I'd keep any vital part of your body for last so you'd feel pain for as long as possible."

Frank whimpered, and the smell coming from him told Jessup his bladder had released. It wasn't a surprise, but Jessup still took a step back, wrinkling his nose.

"Are you done terrorizing the prisoner?" Moore drawled.

Jessup glared at him. "I'll never be done. I don't know what the assassins will do to Frank, but Frank knows I'll come back for him if he ever escapes, right, Frank?" Jessup asked, turning back to Frank.

He was surprised Frank hadn't fainted yet. Sometimes, it happened. The brain of the people he controlled couldn't cope with what was happening, and it shut down. Usually, Jessup felt guilty about it.

Not today.

"We'll take it from here," the man who'd arrived with Dasha said, stepping forward.

Jessup wanted to protest and continue torturing Frank, but he had something better to focus on. So he took a step back, nodding at the man. "Sorry about that," he said.

The man shook his head. "I'd have been pissed, too, if this guy had taken my mate." He paused and grinned. "Maybe you'd like to come over when we interrogate him."

Those words were enough for Frank to lose it. He hadn't fainted before, but he did so now, falling back on the forest ground. No one reached for him to try to stop him, and Jessup winced at the sound Frank's head made when it impacted the ground.

Ouch.

The man who'd arrived with Dasha rolled his eyes. "They're strong as long as they're with their friends but threaten them a bit, and this happens," he said. He offered Jessup his hand. "Roark."

"Jessup. Let me know when you start working him over."

"We will."

There was nothing else Jessup could do. He didn't care what happened to Frank from now on, and while he doubted the assassins would get any answers out of the human, they were welcome to try.

Jessup turned. Rory was standing nearby, his arms wrapped around his body. He had to be cold, which meant Jessup felt guilty for not taking him home as soon as he found him.

"Rory?" he called out gently.

He realized that he'd just shown Rory a side of him his mate hadn't seen before. He was terrified of Rory's reaction, but it was too late to take everything back now. The only thing Jessup could do was wait, and he did so holding his breath.

He almost cried when Rory took a step toward him. When he opened his arms, Rory didn't hesitate to step into them and allow Jessup to wrap them around him. Jessup kissed the top of Rory's head, inhaled his scent, and told himself they were okay.

Rory was safe.

Jessup had known he cared about his mate. How could he not when Rory was offering him everything he could have ever wanted—someone who loved him, someone who would build a family with him eventually, someone to come home to at night after work. Rory was everything Jessup could have dreamed of, and it had become a reality. He might not have realized that before, but when he'd gone back to the rundown structure and had seen that everyone was gone, he'd panicked. He hadn't known what happened to Rory, but he'd been able to feel Rory was freaking out, and that had been enough to tell him that Frank had him. He'd gone after them, and luckily, he'd found them easily enough. In his way, he'd saved Rory, just like Rory had saved him.

Jessup's life could never be complete without Rory. He'd do everything in his power to ensure he never had to experience losing his mate. If that meant beating up hunters, Jessup was all for it.

Rory hadn't expected Jessup to be that lethal, but he'd been impressed. The only Jessup he knew was the gentle one, the soft one who wanted to take care of him and was terrified to lose him.

That wasn't the Jessup Rory had seen just now, but it didn't mean Rory didn't like this side of his mate. He'd been fierce and ready to do anything to protect Rory, which Rory hadn't realized he needed to see. He'd been able to run away from Frank on his own, but it was good to know that if he ever needed it, his mate would have his back. Jessup would ensure no one hurt Rory, and that was all Rory wanted.

"Take me home," he told Jessup. He was cold since he'd ditched the sweater he'd been wearing because it had torn during his shift back.

Jessup turned toward Moore. "Do you need me?"

"No. Teddy, shimmer them to Jessup's room. I'm sure both of them could use a shower."

"I'd kill for a shower," Rory said.

He realized what he'd said and snapped his mouth shut. He didn't think he'd ever be able to kill anyone, no matter how much he wanted to after what Frank had done to him. Still, in his wildest thoughts, he could imagine that instead of running away, he'd faced Frank and had maybe beaten him up.

He quietly snorted to himself. If he'd tried, Frank would no doubt have won.

"Wait," Jessup said, tightening his hold on Rory. "How is Leon?"

"He'll be fine," Dasha explained, stepping closer. "I brought him directly to our infirmary. He's with Jolyn right now, so you don't have to worry about him. Our doctor and Nix will do everything they can. He was already waking up by the time I got him to the infirmary, and Rocco didn't seem too worried."

Rory's knees felt like jelly as he nodded in thanks. He'd been worried about Leon but focused on Jessup and everything else, and he felt slightly guilty about that. Not that Leon would care. Rory might not know him well, but he thought of Leon as a friend, and he suspected Leon would tell him to focus on his mate.

He could do that now.

Teddy looked relieved when he came to stand in front of Jessup. Jessup didn't let go of Rory. He didn't need to, and when he reached for Teddy with one hand, Teddy nodded and took it. He squeezed hard, his knuckles going white.

Rory had never been so glad to have someone shimmer him straight home. Normally, Teddy wouldn't have entered Jessup's bedroom that way because it was a private space, but he'd known what Jessup and Rory needed. He only stayed long enough to make sure they were okay, then he shimmered away, leaving them alone.

Rory finally relaxed. He leaned harder against Jessup's side, and Jessup seemed more than happy to hold his weight.

"Shower?" he asked.

Rory shivered. "Please. I need to wash the feeling of his hands off my skin."

Jessup sucked in a breath. "He didn't touch you, did he?"

"Please, don't make me think about that. No, he just grabbed my arm and pulled me around, but I still hated it."

"Of course he did. Come on. Come take a shower."

Jessup guided Rory toward the bathroom. He made sure Rory had everything he needed before leaving him to it, and while Rory wanted to ask him to stay, he felt especially vulnerable. He needed a few minutes on his own, and as he scrubbed his skin red, he reminded himself that it was over. Frank was gone, and Rory was safe from the labs. He was with his mate, bonded to him.

When Rory stepped out of the shower, he noticed Jessup had left a pile of clothes on the counter in the bathroom. They were too big, but Rory didn't care because they smelled of laundry detergent and Jessup.

Of home.

The feeling solidified when Rory came out of the bathroom. Jessup was hovering close to the door and gestured at his bed as soon as Rory was in sight.

"Why don't you climb in?"

Rory stared. He wanted to obey but felt he was taking Jessup away from something important. "I'm sure you have better things to do than babysit me."

Jessup shook his head. "I don't, and besides, it's not babysitting you. I need to reassure myself that you're okay, and I can't think of a better way to do that than to get into bed with you."

Rory snickered. He suspected Jessup knew what he was thinking about because he grinned. When he kissed the top of Rory's damp hair and gently pushed him toward the bed, Rory didn't hesitate. He allowed Jessup to get him into bed and wrap the blankets around him. Jessup kissed him again, promised he'd be quick and rushed into the bathroom to take the fastest shower anyone had ever taken. Rory could have sworn he was back in under five minutes, and when he did, he smelled of toothpaste and soap.

Rory's heart swelled at the sight of his mate looking so vulnerable with damp hair, bare feet, and pajamas. This was where Rory belonged. He was supposed to be in Jessup's bed and in his life. Bonding had been the first step, and Rory hoped that, eventually, Jessup would be able to trust him with his entire heart.

He hadn't expected that to happen today.

Jessup joined Rory in bed. Rory didn't hesitate to snuggle against him and took his first easy breath since he'd seen Leon bleeding on the ground.

"You're all right?" Jessup asked.

"Never better," Rory confirmed.

Jessup settled deeper into bed, and Rory allowed the warmth of his body and their mixed scents to soothe him.

"When I saw you running away from Frank, I freaked out," Jessup said. "I thought he was going to take you away from me, and I couldn't allow that to happen." He licked his lips. "You're one of the few people who matter to me, and I wouldn't survive losing you."

"You're not going to lose me. I'm not going anywhere." That was a promise, and Rory would die keeping it.

"After I was freed from the lab, I went home," Jessup whispered.

Rory's breath hitched. Was Jessup doing what Rory thought he was doing?

"I thought my parents and siblings would be frantic, but I should have known better," Jessup continued. "They never cared much about me, and we were never close, but I thought they'd have noticed I vanished. I'm pretty sure they did, but when I got to my parents' home, they seemed almost annoyed to see me. They asked what I was doing there, and I told them I'd been freed. They didn't know what I was talking about. They didn't care to find out, either. That's when I realized what had happened. It hurt. I asked them how they could have just washed their hands of me, and once again, they were clueless. They didn't believe me when I told them I was kidnapped and held in a lab. They told me to stop saying stupid things and that if I was going to continue, I needed to leave. So I did. I had nowhere to go, but Moore had made sure we knew how to reach him if we needed to, so that's what I did. I called him, and he and Teddy came to pick me up. I've never been back, and I have no intention of ever doing so."

Rory's eyes burned, but he didn't want to cry. Jessup needed to focus on himself, not on soothing the pain Rory felt at the thought of how Jessup had felt then. "You shouldn't. They don't deserve you or your forgiveness. I'm sorry you had to go through that, but I'm here now, and I'll always look for you if you vanish. You're the other half of my soul. I can't live without you."

Rory was Jessup's, and Jessup was Rory's. That meant something to both of them, even though it hadn't meant much to Jessup's parents. If Jessup was to vanish again, he'd have people look for him. He was loved, even though he hadn't realized it until recently, and Rory would make sure he never forgot it.

Jessup was precious, and Rory would spend years showing him how much, if necessary.

CHAPTER SEVEN

Jessup stared at the house in front of him. It still looked unfinished — the outside needed a coat of paint, the plants had seen better days, and the porch was slightly crooked — but it was his.

Well, theirs. He and Rory were moving in together, and Rikar had been nice enough to offer them this house. He'd refused payment for it, which was a relief because it wasn't like Jessup earned a lot working with the mutants and saving people from the labs. Moore was trying to find a way around that now that more of them were finding mates and partners, but for now, they still relied on Rikar for too much, which made everyone uncomfortable.

Well, except Rikar. He seemed delighted to be able to help, although that might have something to do with the fact that he was Hayes's mate. He'd told Jessup he considered him family since Hayes viewed him as a brother, and Jessup was trying to convince himself that was the truth and that he wasn't imposing.

"Behind you," someone said, startling Jessup out of his thoughts.

He shuffled to the side, allowing Carla to walk past him. She was carrying a box and winked at him as she went.

"I'm not going to do all your work for you," she said with a laugh.

Jessup cleared his throat and turned to grab one of the boxes Teddy had brought over from Rory's apartment. Rory had spent a few days packing his things and getting everything ready. Now, it was moving day. Rory had more things than Jessup, who'd only had a few boxes and a back-pack to move, which meant everyone was focused on his stuff. That was fine with Jessup. He carried the box inside, peeking at the top to find out where he was supposed to put it. This one said kitchen, so he headed that way, smiling at the sound of Rory in there talking to someone.

The smile slipped when Jessup realized Rory was talking to his mother, but Jessup forced himself to walk in anyway. He couldn't avoid the woman forever, since she was his mate's mother. Besides, she'd come to him and apologized for thinking he might be controlling Rory with his ability. Things were okay between them, but they were still wary of each other, and Jessup hoped that feeling would fade in time.

Rory turned to him and beamed. "There you are. I was wondering where you'd ended up."

He slipped an arm around Jessup's waist as soon as Jessup put down the box. He relaxed against Jessup's side, a sure sign he trusted him fully. Sometimes, it still amazed Jessup that Rory had that much faith in him.

He kissed the top of Rory's head, and when he turned to Eliza, it was to find her watching them. She smiled, her expression soft, and Jessup thought that maybe they were headed in the right direction.

"It's so good to see the two of you happy," she said.

"I told you he'd take good care of me," Rory told her.

"And I should have believed you right away. I'm lucky you and Jessup forgave me for what I said."

Jessup was uncomfortable, but Rory's mother was trying, and he needed to do his part. "You were scared for your son. It's entirely understandable, especially after he was kid-napped. I don't hold any of that against you." In fact, it would have been nice to have a mother who worried about him as much as Rory's mom worried about Rory.

But Jessup would never get that. He was making his peace with it, and he was strangely fine with it. It didn't matter that he lost his birth family. Rory and the friends he'd gathered along the way were much more important, and Jessup loved them as much, if not more, as he'd loved his blood family.

"It's a pity you have to move so far away," Rory's mom said.

And there went the peace Jessup had been clinging to. He felt guilty about taking Rory away from his family, no matter how many times Rory told him it was okay. Jessup didn't have his parents and siblings anymore, and he didn't want Rory to lose his.

"You need to stop making Jessup feel guilty," Rory's cousin said as he walked in.

Marcus was carrying a box like Jessup had been earlier, and he put it down on the table. Then he turned to stare at his aunt. "Can't you see he's working himself up again?" he asked, gesturing at Jessup.

Rory's mother looked horrified. "That's not what I meant. You don't need to feel guilty, Jessup. I know Rory will be happy here, probably happier than he was back home. It's just going to be strange, you know? All his life, he was never far from me, and now, he's going to be on the other side of the country."

"And you can visit anytime you want," Rory said, wrapping an arm around her shoulders. "As long as you warn us first."

Rory's mother flushed. "I know better than to come in without letting you know."

That would be because she'd walked into the house just yesterday without knocking, which meant she'd caught Rory and Jessup in the living room trying out the couch, and not for watching TV or sleeping. Jessup felt like he might die every time he thought about it, and while Rory had been embarrassed, too, he'd found it funny.

Jessup, not so much.

"I'm here!" a woman said from the entrance.

Jessup grinned, recognizing Olga's voice. He leaned out the door, relieved to see she seemed to be all right. She'd been spending time with the assassins, trying to find out if Frank knew anything more than he'd already told them, and it was good to have her home.

"We're in the kitchen," Jessup called out.

Olga beamed at him as she came toward him. "I was so happy when Moore told me you were moving in with Rory."

Jessup rolled his eyes. "As if you didn't already know it would happen."

She bumped their shoulders together. "You know, I don't see *everything*."

"But you sure saw Rory."

Olga laughed. "That I did. I knew he was the one for you and that he'd make you happy, and I'm glad I insisted you give him a chance."

They walked into the kitchen. Olga hadn't met Rory's family yet, and it was good to have someone to distract Rory's mother. She was nice, but Jessup still didn't know how to deal with her, and he'd be glad to redirect her attention.

"This is Olga," he said, introducing his friend. "She's kind of the beta of our small mutant pack, but don't let Moore hear you call her that. He doesn't like the alpha thing."

Rory's mother beamed and moved toward Olga. "You helped rescue my son?"

Olga nodded. "I was there when we did."

"I don't know how to thank you." Eliza grabbed Olga and dragged her into a hug, surprising everyone.

From the way both women tensed, Jessup could tell something was happening. He frowned, but he couldn't tell what was going on. From the outside, it was just a hug between two women who didn't know each other.

Olga staggered back, her hand flying to her mouth as she stared at Eliza. "I didn't see this," she murmured.

"What do you mean?" Eliza asked. She looked as shocked as Olga.

Olga licked her lips. "I see the future. That's my ability. I never saw you coming, though."

Eliza smiled and reached for Olga. "That's fine. I'm Eliza."

Olga took Eliza's hand. They were looking at each other in a peculiar way, and Jessup peered at his mate, wondering if he saw the same thing. Rory was frowning, staring at his mother, and he clearly could tell something was happening.

"Mom?" he asked.

Eliza turned to Rory. "I don't think you'll be the only one to move here."

Rory groaned. "We already talked about it. I don't want you to move here just because I am."

Eliza laughed. "I'm sorry, but you won't be the one I'm moving for." She turned to Olga. "My mate is."

It took Jessup a second to understand what Eliza was saying. When he did, he gaped, staring at the two women.

"Seriously?" Rory asked, sounding like he didn't quite believe them.

Olga's smile was everything. "Seriously." She grinned wickedly. "Hey, Jessup. Looks like I'm your new mother-in-law."

Jessup groaned. She'd hold that over his head forever, dammit.

ABOUT THE AUTHOR

Catherine is the creator of several series, most of them paranormal, including the Whitedell Pride Series and the Gillham
Pack Series. While she graduated in translation, she decided
to go the writer's way because it was more fun to create her
own stories and characters.

She's been living in Italy for more than twenty years, but
she's a daughter of the North—Belgium to be precise—and
she misses it so much that she's already planning to move
back.

She loves pizza—probably too much—her son, her pets,
and of course, books. She sneaks some reading time into her
schedule every time she has five minutes free from writing,
demands from her various pets and son, and lastly, house-
work.

Connect with her:

lievens.catherine@gmail.com
BookBub: https://www.bookbub.com/authors/catherine-
lievens
Website: https://authorcatherinelievens.com/
Facebook: https://www.facebook.com/catherine.lievens.9
Facebook Group: https://www.facebook.com/groups/
411788002341528/
Twitter: https://twitter.com/authorCLievens
Newsletter: http://eepurl.com/c-uvKn

www.ingramcontent.com/pod-product-compliance
Lightning Source LLC
Chambersburg PA
CBHW060635130626
46555CB00002B/807